Puzzle Man

David B. McKinney

7710-T Cherry Park Dr, Ste 224
Houston, TX 77095
(713) 766-4271

Printed in the United States of America

ISBN: 9781684118656

Praise for

Quest for Closure

Compelling storyline... a rollercoaster ride of emotions.

– OnlineBookClub.org

The Invisible Four

Remarkable plot and twisty-turning nature.

– RedheadedBookLover.com

Dedication

This book is dedicated to my parents, Patricia and the late Robert McKinney, and my late mother- and father-in-law, Jackie and George Mefferd. They each exemplified aging gracefully with dignity. I also dedicate this book to Jack Gibson, a retired Air Force pilot who served during World War II, the Korean and Vietnam wars. Jack and I became good friends while I was a hospice volunteer in the final months of his 97 years on earth.

To the dedicated staffs at Harbor Place in Gig Harbor, Wash., Canterbury Park in Longview, Wash., and other senior living communities coast to coast, the care and love you provide are much appreciated.

Finally, to the men and women in senior living communities, their families and friends, I hope you find the story of Kenny Boone to be entertaining, relevant and compelling. Kenny is a fictional character, but his circumstances are very real.

A Brief History of Crossword Puzzles

Crossword puzzles are said to be the most popular and widespread word game in the world yet have a short history. The first crosswords appeared in England during the 19th century. They were of an elementary kind, apparently derived from the word square, a group of words arranged so the letters read alike vertically and horizontally and printed in children's puzzle books and various periodicals. In the United States, however, the puzzle developed into a serious adult pastime.

The first known published crossword puzzle was a "Word-Cross Puzzle" created by a journalist named Arthur Wynne from Liverpool, and he is usually credited as the inventor of the popular word game. December 21, 1913 was the date it appeared in a Sunday newspaper, the *New York World*.

– George Eliot

Are You a Cruciverbalist?

A cruciverbalist is someone who constructs or enjoys solving crossword puzzles. Inventor Arthur Wynne's first puzzle was designed as a diamond shape. A few weeks after this Word-Cross appeared, the name of the puzzle was changed to "Cross-Word" as a result of a typesetting error.

Although Wynne's invention was initially greeted with skepticism, by the 1920s it had established itself as a popular activity, entertaining and frustrating generations of cruciverbalists.

Chapter 1

"Eat up, Dad, 'cause we're taking a drive," Sarah said. "And in case you're wondering, you aren't driving."

Kenny Boone, 84, swallowed a bite of sandwich and asked if this was his last meal, so to speak. His daughter didn't answer, but the look in her eyes told Kenny that he might be on the right track. He finished his lunch while Sarah scurried around tidying the kitchen.

"Where are we going?" Kenny said as they drove along the Galveston Seawall Boulevard. "You do realize I'm not a surfer, never was."

"I'm not taking you surfing, hunting for seashells or to build sandcastles. Enjoy the scenery, we're almost there. I know you're going to love it."

Kenny didn't love it one damn bit. The understated signage outside the main entrance of the sprawling complex read *Gulf Breeze of Galveston — A Senior Living Community*. Through clenched teeth, Kenny stared out the car window while Sarah hustled around to open the passenger door. Reluctantly, he got out and stood like a statue. He was greeted by a barrage of chirping from an enthusiastic young woman wearing a name tag that identified her as *Lucy – Family Care Director*. She ushered them into the lobby to escape the glaring sun. Only when Lucy stopped talking did Kenny snap out of his deep thoughts. He smiled at Lucy and turned to his daughter.

"So, Sarah, you're moving your old man to his final resting place... or next to final. Have you given up on me?"

"No, Dad, I only want what's best for you. How could you say such a thing? You need to live at a place that can look after you better than I can."

An awkward moment of silence followed. The thrumming of the AC seemed particularly loud. Finally, Kenny mumbled something about knowing that Sarah was just trying to do the right thing. Still...

"I've never been very good at being alone. When your mother died, I had moments when I didn't think I could continue without her. But you took me in and that was so thoughtful of you. Now, I feel alone again."

Sarah had heard this all before, of course. It would only start an argument if she reminded her father that he tended to repeat himself. Kenny would deny it and accuse her of not listening. Fact of the matter was his dementia affected all aspects of his behavior, which was why she could no longer care for him at home.

Sarah forced a smile and held her father's hand as Lucy gave them a tour of the facility. It was impressive: two dining rooms, a game room, TV room, exercise room, library, coffee lounge or bistro, outdoor courtyard and more. A shuttle van parked out front took residents to the doctor, shopping, and on other excursions.

The one-bedroom second floor unit Lucy took them to had a balcony with an ocean view. The kitchen was compact yet functional, and the newish carpet was plush. Sarah could see herself living quite comfortably at Gulf Breeze but wasn't sure she'd ever willingly give up her home.

"Well, Dad, what do you think?" said Sarah.

Kenny sighed and admitted the place was nice. He knew where this was heading and decided to stop giving Sarah a hard time. She loved him and deserved more out of life than babysitting her old man.

"I'm willing to give it a shot, that's all I will commit to today. Who knows, I might even like it here. Then again... "

Sarah gave her dad a big hug and exchanged smiles with Lucy during the embrace. Finally, a breakthrough. She took Kenny by the arm and promised him a shrimp dinner at his favorite seafood restaurant.

"Lucy, I'll bring my dad back on Monday to move in. See you then."

Kenny whispered something about selling his soul for a shrimp dinner. Sarah ignored the comment and busied herself with buckling him in for the ride to the restaurant and then home. His current home, that is. Not to be confused with this new home at Gulf Breeze.

Chapter 2

Monday arrived and with it came a gnawing in Kenny's gut. He'd transferred all over the world during his time in the Air Force and hadn't ever felt so uncertain about his future. The military provided instant companionship and camaraderie; loneliness eventually lessened or vanished. This, however, was different.

"Ready to go, Dad?" said Sarah. "All of your personal stuff is stowed in the truck. You want to drive it to Gulf Breeze?"

"Yeah, I want to drive. Promise me you won't sell my truck while I'm being institutionalized."

"You are a curmudgeon, no doubt about that," Sarah replied. "I don't plan on selling your truck so you can rest your mind. And another thing, assisted living is a far cry from a mental hospital or prison, so stop whining."

Kenny explained for the umpteenth time how much his life had changed in the past few years: he lost Rebecca to cancer, most of his friends had died or were in a home, he was relinquishing the keys to his truck, and Sarah was evicting (his word choice) and moving him to an old folks' stockade with soft food and bingo.

"I swear that being around you lately is just plain depressing. Do you ever listen to what you're saying?"

"You know me, Sarah. My bark is worse than my bite. I wear my feelings on my sleeve for the world to see. It's how I cope."

Sarah emitted an exasperated harrumph. "Get in the truck, Mr. Grumpy. See if you can get us to Gulf Breeze without causing another Silver Alert."

Kenny shot her a look. The most recent Silver Alert had been his third in a year.

Lucy was standing just inside the main entrance when Kenny and Sarah arrived at Gulf Breeze. She had a roller cart ready for Kenny's belongings and wasted little time in unloading the truck. Sarah smiled and crooked her finger at Kenny, indicating he was to hand over the truck keys. His frown was to be expected. He dangled the keys and she snatched them away.

Kenny tuned out the chit-chat between Lucy and Sarah during the walk and elevator ride to 258, the same room he'd visited a few days earlier. Where it had been empty before, it now had a double bed and chest of drawers, a small dining table with two chairs, a couch, recliner, and color TV. Boxes of bedding, towels, kitchenware and other items were stacked in a corner. Sarah had been busy over the weekend.

"Do you want me to help you unpack, Daddy?"

Kenny shook his head and told Sarah he'd handle it. "It'll take me about an hour to get situated. That will leave me with the rest of my life minus sixty minutes to fill."

Lucy chuckled, "You're going to wonder where the time goes at Gulf Breeze, Mr. Boone. There is so much to do here. But if you don't feel like it, you'll find it is excellent for quiet time."

Sarah stood at the large window and said she'd love to recline on the balcony reading and gazing at the Gulf. Lucy said at any given moment, a fair number of residents are on their balconies doing just that.

"I bet it's exciting to watch a hurricane coming ashore," said Kenny. "If you have a death wish, that is."

"I'm glad you mentioned hurricanes," said Lucy. This facility took a mild beating during Hurricane Harvey in 2017 and Ike in 2008. It was built with hurricanes and tropical storms in mind. No guarantees, you understand, but we're confident that Gulf Breeze can withstand major storms."

Lucy headed for the door. "Dinner is served between five and six-thirty each evening, and your table is number 14, Mr. Boone. You'll like your table mates–I found just the right threesome for you. See you later!"

Kenny watched her go and turned to Sarah. "I'll be okay, you run along, too. But before you go, answer me one question: Did you put me on the second floor for a reason? This place has four levels. You hoping to avoid a worst-case scenario?"

"If you think you're being funny now, you're not. I'll be back tomorrow. Try to have a positive outlook."

Kenny slumped into the recliner and softly said to the empty room that all he was positive about was he probably wouldn't like it at Gulf Breeze.

God help me. My daughter is right. I am a grumpy SOB.

Chapter 3

Kenny skipped dinner his first night at Gulf Breeze, instead choosing to munch on crackers and watch a rerun of *American Ninja Warrior*. He got up early the next morning and found a large coffee urn just inside the dining room. He poured himself a cup and wandered out into the main level hallway. He remembered from the tour that the game room was nearby. It was empty except for a uniformed housekeeper who dropped a rolled up copy of *The Daily News* onto the large card table. She smiled at Kenny and hurried off.

Sipping coffee (not bad), Kenny glanced at the front page and sports section headlines. He'd get back to the articles in due course. First, he wanted to check out today's crossword puzzle. He helped himself to a Ticonderoga #2 from an old cigar box of pens and pencils.

Time seemed to stand still while Kenny worked the puzzle. Kind of like his periodic fogs, he thought to himself. Kenny's routine at home–*Sarah's* home–was to make a quick pass at the easy clues, refill his coffee cup and then return for the home stretch. Although he didn't keep score, Kenny figured his success rate at completing the entire daily puzzle without looking up clues was about 70 percent. The clues involving foreign languages, Shakespeare and classical music regularly stumped him.

Table 14 was adjacent to one of the floor-to-ceiling windows with a partial view of the Gulf on a clear day. Kenny walked by the table and eyeballed the two men eating breakfast. They looked at him expectantly and appeared disappointed when he didn't join them. Apparently, they'd been told of their new table mate and were anxious for him to join them. Kenny got his coffee and walked back to the game room. He felt eyes on him, but looked straight ahead until he was seated once again.

Sixty minutes later Kenny rose from his seat and stretched. He'd completed the puzzle, which he took to be a good omen. Day one at Gulf Breeze and he was batting a thousand. With a slight spring in his step, Kenny went back to his room and finished unpacking the boxes of personal items. Hungry, he scrounged up something from the pantry and made a mental note to go down to lunch. If he waited until just before the dining room closed, he might be able to avoid his curious table mates.

The knock on the door startled Kenny. It was Lucy, as bubbly as ever.

"Hello, Mr. Boone. I saw you in the game room this morning. Finding your way around so far?"

"Yeah, I paid attention when you gave the tour. By the way, your badge reads *Family Care Director*. Where do I fit in? It's only me."

Lucy said he now was part of the Gulf Breeze family as were all residents. She went on to describe the day's itinerary, emphasizing how everything was optional. There were arts and crafts at ten, a shuttle ride to a mall right after lunch, bingo at four, and a sing-along at seven-thirty.

"I don't know if you're a *Jeopardy!* fan; if you are, you'll need to get to the TV room early to get a good seat. Residents love Alex Trebek and *Jeopardy!*"

Kenny told her he'd never been a fan of game shows. Sports were more his thing.

"I can almost guarantee that within six months you'll be hooked on *Jeopardy!* That's what happens here," she said. "I'm taping a calendar of the activities this month on your refrigerator. Be sure to check the easel in the lobby for any changes day-to-day."

Kenny nodded and held the door open for her. She took the hint. He pulled the calendar from the refrigerator and took it to the balcony. It was a beautiful day and the aroma of the Gulf was invigorating. Yes, there were a lot of activities at his new facility, but were they for him? Was he a bingo kind of guy? He felt a wave of loneliness wash over him and closed his eyes. The events calendar slipped from his hand and fluttered over the railing.

I don't know if I can do this.

Diary: January 21

This is my first diary entry since moving to Gulf Breeze. First one ever, actually. For the record, it isn't my idea; Dr. Kim says doing this will help with my dementia. I agreed to jot down my feelings occasionally, which I define as whenever I feel like it. I don't have a fancy bound diary like they sell at the mall. I dug out my vintage Underwood manual typewriter, replaced the ribbon, bought a ream of cheap paper, and am good to go.

I'll begin with the circumstances that led to my life sentence to Gulf Breeze. I'm using first person, present tense as if I'm talking to others in a therapy group. Dr. Kim knows I'm not the type to bare my soul to strangers. This is the next best thing. Here goes.

Why am I trudging along the side of this busy road? There are an awful lot of motorcyclists roaring by–Harley's I would guess, by the sound of loud exhaust pipes. Lots of yelling and honking, too. A parade? Maybe it's spring break and the young people are letting off steam. Maybe not. I can't even recall what month it is.

My feet, or dogs as my old man called them, are sore. I need to get where I'm going soon, or my barking dogs will wake up the neighbors. I know, that's kind of corny. The problem is I don't know where I'm headed. Hopefully I'll figure it out by the time I get there. I should have stayed with my pickup truck. I could have rolled up the windows and turned on the radio to mask the noise of traffic. And my dogs wouldn't be barking.

I'm an honest man and especially honest with myself. I try to BS some people, but that doesn't work when it's me I want to fool.

Dementia's a cruel bitch. I know that the frequency and duration of my "lapses" are increasing. Lapses are how Dr. Lee describes my memory issues. I call the lapses "fogs" because they remind me of fog rolling in from the Gulf of Mexico, obscuring my clear thoughts. I can't predict where or when a fog will arrive and leave me temporarily clueless. I think this is one of those times, otherwise why would I vacate a perfectly good truck to walk to... somewhere?

The bench up ahead affords a clear view of the ocean. It's as good a place as any to take a load off and close my eyes for a few minutes. The bench is unoccupied so I can stretch out in comfort. Relief is on the way. If I had a "Do Not Disturb" sign like they have at motel rooms, I'd hang it around my neck.

The best I can hope for is that when I awaken, it'll come to me why I'm here. It always has before. Well, not always. In fact, I may never know. I'm old and falling apart. See you on the other side.

Chapter 4

One seat was empty at table 14 when Kenny went down to dinner. His self-imposed exile wasn't working, and it was time to move on from crackers and cookies. There was one open place at his table; two men and a woman were already seated. Kenny sat down and nodded at the other three.

"I saw you here at breakfast," one of the men said. "When you didn't stop by, I assumed you weren't the new guy joining us. By the way, I'm Jack, affectionately known as Blackjack. This is my wife, Maisey, and that gentleman is Frank."

"Hi, everyone. My name is Kenny, affectionately known as Kenny. You're right, I'm the new guy. The food here any good?"

Frank shrugged his shoulders and said it grew on you. "I don't know how it is with you, Kenny, but as I get older my appetite decreases. I used to shovel in the meat and potatoes. Now, the joy of eating is over. I pick at my food and eat enough to stay alive."

Kenny looked at Maisey who had not yet spoken. She moved her lips but the sound she emitted was unintelligible. Before he could ask her to repeat herself, Blackjack interjected.

"Maisey had a stroke two years ago and has a hard time talking. FYI, her mind is sharp and there's nothing wrong with her hearing."

Kenny glanced at Maisey's left hand and saw the gold wedding band. His eyes darted to Blackjack's ring finger and saw a matching men's version. Well, Blackjack had said they were married. Kenny had never expected to come across a mixed-race couple this late in life. She was as white as Blackjack was black.

A young waiter hovered politely nearby until the table talk ceased. He offered coffee or tea and recited the menu of oatmeal, toast, fruit cup and sliced cantaloupe. Choose any or all of the items, he explained. Kenny chose all, which elicited a slight smile from Maisey.

Kenny was cordial during the meal. He asked enough questions to be polite. When things were winding down, he asked Blackjack how he got his nickname. Was he a gambler, perhaps?

Blackjack leaned back in his cheer and carefully dabbed the corners of his mouth with a napkin.

"No, I'm not much of a gambler unless you consider the risks I take eating the 'cooks choice' entrees they have here. That's code for leftovers, just so you know. Anyway, my moniker dates to my childhood in Tulsa where I was the only African-American in my neighborhood. Need another hint?"

All eyes were on Kenny. He mulled over what he'd heard and then it came to him: the boy's name was Jack and he was black. Blackjack.

"So, if I call you Blackjack, would you be offended?" Kenny said.

"My friends call me Blackjack," he said with a smile. "You're on probation for thirty days. If, after a month, we've become friends, then Blackjack it is. Until then I'm plain old Jack."

Kenny rose and bid his new table mates a good evening. He got a caffeine-free coffee to go and returned to his room for night.

The next morning Kenny was up early and in the game room by seven. He noticed right away that something was wrong. The daily newspaper had been folded such that the crossword puzzle was on top of the stacked sections. Furthermore, a row of squares had letters in them. Obviously, someone else had beat him to the punch that morning. In Kenny's mind, that meant he'd have to get up even earlier to be sure he had first access to the newspaper.

Lucy was passing by in the hallway and saw Kenny standing at the card table.

"Hey, Mr. Boone, good morning to you. I'm glad to see you venturing from your room."

"One day at a time," said Kenny. "You happen to know how many copies of *The Daily News* are delivered here? I only see one."

Lucy told him just the one copy. They used to get several, but people didn't seem interested. It was an easy budget cut.

"More and more residents rely on their mobile phones and tablets to get caught up on local and world events," she said. TV news is still popular, especially the weather alerts during hurricane season. The daily newspaper though? Not so much."

Kenny turned his attention to the newspaper and scrutinized the puzzle. Lucy took that as her cue to exit. Reading from top to bottom was *me;* left to right was *help. Me help?* Obviously, it was *help me.*

It made no sense to Kenny. It had to be some kind of joke. He whipped his head around to see if anyone was watching and only observed a man and woman shuffling along the hallway, heads down and sniping at each other.

Perhaps it was a one-time thing by a bored resident. A doodler of sorts, he wondered. Kenny pushed the newspaper aside and told himself he'd start fresh in the morning. Let Mr. or Ms. Help Me have today's puzzle. He'd be back bright and early tomorrow to reclaim what he quickly came to consider as his domain.

The daily puzzle belonged to Kenny Boone.

So, it's come down to this: three boxes, a couple of suitcases and a small pile of shirts, pants, and jackets on hangers. This is your life, Kenny Boone. Hah, pathetic. I got rid of a lot of stuff when I moved in with Sarah two years ago. That was one of her conditions for taking me in. Funny thing is I barely remember what I gave away or tossed out.

I'm glad I hung onto my collection of framed photographs. The walls in my Gulf Breeze unit need decorating. This photo of me with six other guys is special. I was their crew chief when we were based at Ramstein Air Base in Germany. Man, that was a long time ago. I'd just made staff sergeant with the 435th Air Ground Operations Wing. I loved that job. Heck, I loved almost all of my postings in the Air Force and that's saying a lot considering I put in thirty-four years.

Here's a photo from my wedding day. I was only eighteen and had just completed basic training. It was early 1953 and the Korean War was winding down. Rebecca was radiant... some sixty-five years before cancer took her away from me. And this one, of Rebecca, baby Sarah and me. Right out of central casting. To think that girl grew up to take care of me is mind-boggling. Not the way it should be, but fairly common I'm told.

These photo enlargements from Arizona are special. In our younger days the three of us would vacation in Sedona and Flagstaff. We hiked miles so that I could get the beautiful shots that ended up on our living room walls. Those will look spectacular when I get them hung.

What did I just say? Guess I'm accepting the fact that I have moved on. I study that family photo and know in my heart that Sarah's difficult decision to move me to assisted living is based on love. Tough love. She told me the recent Silver Alert was quite painful for her. She'd let her imagination go wild with various scenarios of my fate. Can't blame her for using that escapade as the proverbial straw that broke the camel's back to get me full-time adult supervision.

Okay, about done here. All that's left are these stacks of crossword puzzle books. I got hooked on puzzles in the Air Force. Some of the guys played cards, read or slept. Crossword puzzles occupied my mind on lengthy deployments and to this day are how I choose to fill down time.

Dr. Lee says that mental stimulation helps defer dementia. Who knew? I still have my fogs or lapses, though, like parking my truck, walking for hours and being the subject of a Silver Alert. Maybe I should do more crosswords? Unlikely. I do enough as it is.

I hear a housekeeper in the hallway humming a Rolling Stones song while she tidies up. Sounds like "Sympathy for the Devil." Prophetic?

Chapter 5

Kenny was enjoying a quiet moment in the courtyard when he heard a chair scrape against the cobblestone patio. It was Frank, one of his table 14 mates.

"I saw you out here by yourself. If you want me to leave just say so. I understand about having solitary time to think things over."

Kenny's long stint in the Air Force taught him to size up people quickly. First impressions were almost always on the money. He liked what he saw in Frank, himself a retired Marine. They had an immediate bond from their military careers.

"Happy to have you join me," said Kenny. "I'd just finished my serious thinking for the day and was about to doze off. You rescued me from snoring and drooling."

It turned out that when Frank's wife died eight months earlier, he stayed at Gulf Breeze, citing he had nowhere else to go–his adult children resided out of state. Like Kenny, Frank had moved countless times in the service and was content to stay put.

"That's my story, Kenny. How'd you end up here?"

Kenny figured that telling Frank his story would make it easier later when he made an entry in his diary. Practice makes perfect and all of that. He cleared his throat and began.

"The Silver Alert went out over local radio and television stations. It didn't take long to get results. Activation of the public notification system for missing persons always generated a fair amount of responses from folks who swore they spotted the person in question; more often than not, those concerned citizens who called the hotline number weren't much help to the police. Still, every call warrants consideration. One caller did indeed earn good deed status by late afternoon."

Kenny paused and finished the iced tea he was nursing. He glanced at Frank and still had his attention.

"Sgt. Murphy from the Galveston Police Department called Sarah. He said the Silver Alert had turned up yours truly; I was okay physically, just dehydrated and sunburned. Sarah was to go to the main station when she got the message.

"I was picked up by a young patrolman at a seaside bench about three miles from where I'd parked my truck hours earlier–rather poorly the cop mentioned. He said it was a miracle another vehicle hadn't clipped the pickup's jutting rear bumper."

"A miracle you weren't hit by a speeding motorist, more like it," said Frank.

Kenny collected his thoughts and continued.

"I was tired, thirsty, and dazed. Sarah arrived at the station and was upset, as you'd expect. She'd been there, done that when it came to retrieving me–I'd gone missing twice before.

"It dawned on me later how traumatic this was for Sarah. Her husband had moved out a year ago, forcing her to resume her career as a dental hygienist. I think the strain of being my caretaker pushed hubby out the door.

"I remember Sarah's final task before turning in the night she retrieved me from the police was to set the house alarm. I grimaced when I realized the alarm had more to do with keeping me in than keeping a burglar out."

Frank stood and flexed his knees. "Why you did park you truck and walk away? Where were you going?"

"Beats me. It only makes sense when you consider my dementia and memory lapses or fogs," said Kenny. "I don't see the fogs coming and when I have one, I have little or no recollection of what I did. Hell, I could have killed someone for all I know."

Frank sat down again. "Did you?"

Chapter 6

Kenny was fumbling with the TV remote when Sarah knocked lightly and entered his room. She looked at him, her mind flashing back to the days when he was a vibrant, active man. Now he was rapidly approaching the "shell of his old self" she read about in online Alzheimer's chat rooms.

"Daddy, are you busy?" she said quietly. He put the remote on the coffee table and swore softly.

"Well, if you call wasting time trying to record a movie busy, then yes, I'm busy," he said. "Sit down, you make me nervous standing there."

Sarah sat next to him and asked if he wanted her to turn on the radio or record the movie for him. He declined. She then offered to open the blinds to let in sunlight; it was a beautiful day. No to that, as well.

"Listen, Dad, I understand you're not happy being in this place. And I know you're mad at me for moving you here. But it's been almost three months. You need to get on with your life."

Kenny cleared his throat and looked out the window. He thought he'd done a good job at hiding his depression. Apparently not... Sarah was on to him.

"Speaking of moving, I'm unhappy that you moved me here," said Kenny. "If you want to make things right between us, move me back home."

Sarah explained again how she was ill-equipped to manage his growing need for personal care. The last Silver Alert was one too many. She couldn't continue worrying about the periodic fogs he was experiencing. It was just too much.

Kenny lowered his head and bit his lower lip. Sarah wondered if the tough old bird was fighting back tears

"Dad, tell me something. You won't turn on the radio or TV, you sit here in the dark too much and the staff tells me you rarely socialize with the other residents. You isolate yourself in the game room with crossword puzzles. What goes through your mind?"

"I don't think about anything... my mind is blank. I enjoy the solitude and waiting in silence."

Sarah sighed. "Waiting for what? I can't move you back home, I've told you that."

Kenny looked at Sarah and uttered, "What do you think?"

Now it was Sarah's turn to tear up. As she backed out of the room, she saw her father's eyes close and chin rest upon his chest.

"I love you, Daddy."

She hesitated a moment, hoping, but there was no reply from Kenny... she had to settle for the dull, metallic sound of the door latching behind her.

Kenny was spiraling downward. Sarah met with Dr. Kim who shared with her the results of a recent examination.

Her father's age-related dementia was evident in his memory loss, forgetfulness, and confusion. His cognitive functions of thinking and reasoning were stable for the time being. Dr. Kim could tell from Sarah's expression that none of this was new information.

"One in ten men in the U.S. living past age 55 will develop some form of dementia," she pointed out. "That computes to almost six million men and women who are living with dementias, 70 percent of them due to Alzheimer's disease."

"Wow, those numbers are staggering," said Sarah. "My research showed that the explosion of Alzheimer's and dementia (AD) the past few decades is directly related to longer life expectancy. You live long enough, I heard George Burns say on his 100th birthday, you're going to get sick and die of something."

Dr. Kim chuckled. She acknowledged that some people are genetically predisposed to show signs of AD as they age. Others have health conditions known to be associated with an increased risk of getting AD like high blood pressure, high cholesterol, vascular disease, obesity, and smoking, to name a few.

"Your dad is a typical example of someone whose AD symptoms emerged around 80 and have steadily taken hold of his life. In many respects, he is a 'normal' 84-year-old who has a common affliction of the elderly."

Sarah and Dr. Kim discussed Kenny's regimen of medications. The doctor made one adjustment and said she'd pass on the change to the medical staff at Gulf Breeze. She said she'd continue to confer with Gulf Breeze and Sarah about Kenny's condition and behavior and stay on the monthly examination schedule until further notice.

"Sarah, I know from our talks that you feel helpless watching your father decline. Moving him to a senior living community has been traumatic for you both. So, I'm giving you an assignment. You up for it?"

"Yes, I need something to do with my father besides checking in on him every few days. So far, it's been rather depressing."

Dr. Kim outlined a four-point plan for her father. It was up to Sarah to fill in the blanks for each section, including a daily timeline of activities, goals, and notes on Kenny's prevailing outlook on life. There was a wealth of related information online, she assured Sarah.

Number one on the list was a healthful diet. Dr. Kim wasn't concerned about Kenny getting foods rich in B complex vitamins, anti-inflammatories and unsaturated fats. Gulf Breeze was on top of dietary requirements and restrictions for all of its residents. Even the caffeine content of coffee served in the dining room and bistro was monitored. Sarah's task was to monitor her father's between-meal snacks.

"Easier said than done. My father is known for stashing Oreos and licorice around the house. He's a 'sneaky snacker.'"

Number two was regular physical exercise. Sarah didn't expect her dad to readily join the group fitness sessions at Gulf Breeze, but as long as he could walk... he needed to walk. About 5,000 steps a day was recommended, plus aerobic and resistance exercises twice a week. The staff trainer could customize a plan for Kenny.

The third item in Dr. Kim's plan was to find opportunities for Kenny to lower stress. Medication helped manage stress, but it wasn't the total answer. Two favorites for elderly were the moving meditation of tai chi and breath awareness meditation. Finally, Kenny would greatly benefit from increased socialization. Sarah couldn't agree more. Studies had shown that friendships could improve one's mental, physical and emotional health by addressing loneliness, isolation and depression. Kenny was a prime candidate for developing bonds with his new neighbors. Although an avid crossword puzzle solver, which got him out of his room and offered limited cognitive and stress-reduction benefits, it was done in isolation. The same could be said for his diary entries. Kenny needed to mingle and interact, the doctor advised.

"I don't know how you're going to pull off this plan, but just know that any progress is a victory," said Dr. Kim. "Set small, achievable goals. Don't overwhelm your father with too much too soon. I am anxious to hear your report next month."

Sarah's head was spinning on her drive home. She couldn't wait to have a cup of tea and begin outlining the details of the four-point plan.

"Dad," she said to herself as she pulled into the drive-way, "I'm not letting you go down without a fight. You taught me to be strong as a little girl and now it's my turn to help you return to be the Kenny Boone we both miss."

Chapter 7

"Hey, Puzzle Man, haven't seen you at meals for a while. You on one of those trendy diets the Hollywood stars rave about?"

Blackjack grinned at Kenny, who noticed that Maisey and Frank also wore amused expressions.

"I've been busy," said Kenny. "And what did you call me? Puzzle Man?"

Frank held up his palm. "Don't take it the wrong way. It's kind of funny, really. You've been here a few months and hardly anyone knows your name. We've all seen you hunched over the crossword puzzle every morning. Someone tagged you Puzzle Man and it stuck."

"I kind of like it," said Blackjack. "It beats the hell out of my nickname. That reminds me, your probationary period is over and you can now call me Blackjack. Welcome to the elite club."

Kenny looked around the dining room, sighed, and shook his head. So, he thought to himself, I have a nickname. Puzzle Man. A bit boring, but descriptive and much more politically correct than the moniker I earned in the Air Force during a wild weekend on leave.

"Puzzle Man, eh? I can live with that name," Kenny said. "And Blackjack, you can call me Puzzle Man–no probationary period required."

After putting away a bowl of oatmeal and slice of toast, Kenny returned to the game room with a cup of coffee. He settled in and was immediately agitated. Someone had filled in answer squares again. As usual, it was intersecting horizontal and vertical spaces. The message was another cry for help; that is, if it was legitimate and not a jokester messing with Puzzle Man. *Time* was written left to right, and *is near* began with the *i* in time and ran up and down the puzzle. The earlier messages had to do with wanting and needing help, while the tone of this one was more foreboding. *Time is near.* Kenny was intrigued. This was a puzzle within a puzzle. What was going to happen?

Kenny strolled the long hallways of Gulf Breeze. Taking walks to shake out the cobwebs dated to his early days as an airplane mechanic at MacDill Air Force Base near Tampa. Several people said hello to Kenny as he passed by, but he was too absorbed in thought about the mysterious puzzler to make a connection with his neighbors. His detachment only cemented his growing reputation as a loner who preferred puzzles to people.

At one point, it could have been fifteen minutes or five hours, Kenny had enough walking and headed for his room. He was on the third floor and his room was on the second floor. Kenny kept walking with the expectation that if he walked long enough he'd end up outside the correct unit.

"Mr. Boone, Mr. Boone, wake up." Lucy gently shook Kenny's shoulder.

"What's the matter? Is there a problem?"

Lucy assured Kenny that there was no major problem; however, anxious calls from third floor residents to the front desk did trigger a quick reaction.

"The first call reported that a man was asleep in the hallway," said Lucy. "That was followed by another call which described the sleeping person as Puzzle Man. You're Puzzle Man, aren't you Mr. Boone?"

Kenny got to his feet a little disheveled and a lot embarrassed. He told Lucy he's the one and only Puzzle Man. A small crowd had gathered in the hallway. Kenny noted their curiosity and concern.

"I was on my way to my room and the next thing I remember is being awakened by you, Lucy," Kenny said. "Sorry if I caused a scene. I didn't mean to scare anyone."

An elderly woman said Kenny looked so peaceful she didn't want to disturb him. Her husband blurted that you can't ignore a man sleeping outside your door.

"You did the right thing in calling the desk," said Lucy. "Obviously Mr. Boone got confused, sat down to rest and fell asleep. Come on, I'll take you to your room."

On the slow walk to room 258 Kenny confessed to Lucy that he recalled nothing after leaving the game room. When Lucy asked if he had experienced a memory lapse or fog, he nodded.

"Yes, this is just like the other fogs. I walk somewhere and then fall asleep. Lucky, I didn't go to the roof and take a header by mistake. Sarah made a good call in taking away my truck keys."

"Big difference between having a fog episode at Gulf Breeze and out in busy traffic," Lucy pointed out. "Look around, we have cameras everywhere. Safety and security are our top priorities. You only slept five minutes before I arrived on the third floor."

Kenny couldn't believe it. That meant that between walking the halls and sleeping he'd been out of commission for more than an hour. Sarah would be happy to hear how much exercise he got today. She could put it in her report for Dr. Kim. Neither would be pleased to hear that the episodes were becoming more frequent.

This latest fog was his second in three weeks.

Diary: March 2

I've got to get a grip on what's happening to me. It'd make a world of difference if only I could feel a fog coming on. Even a five-minute-warning would give me time to get to my room where I could wait it out in my recliner or bed. No need to put on a show for the residents of Gulf Breeze. If they want live entertainment, they can play bingo.

Dr. Kim, God bless her, tried to explain my condition in a way I could follow. She caught herself a few times using big words. The gist of it is my form of dementia is irreversible. Diet, exercise, meds, and the rest are helpful in delaying worst-case, but in the long run the symptoms will increase in frequency and duration. The day will come when I won't have the ability to recall I had a fog. At that stage it's hasta la vista, Boone.

I am a fighter, always have been. The Air Force taught me how to survive in demanding circumstances all over the world. As a master sergeant, I was equally adept at giving and taking orders. I could be a hard-ass, probably still am. What I can't take, what I'm struggling with right now, is not being in total control of myself.

As it turns out, one of my table mates, Frank, is into computers. He says he doesn't do Facebook or anything like that, even though his grandchildren beg him to. What he loves is to look up stuff on Google and Wikipedia. He carries around a small notebook and jots down names, places, dates, etc. and then goes to the library at Gulf Breeze to snag one of the computers. He methodically goes through his list and when he finds what he wants on the computer about one item, moves on to the next.

I had Frank do me a favor, seeing how we're both vets. The former Marine... correction, there is no such thing as a former Marine... researched dementia for me. He came back with a thick stack of printed pages. Most were from the AARP web site. Some of the factoids include: more than 380,000 Texans are living with Alzheimer's disease/dementia. It's the sixth leading cause of death in America and it kills more people than breast and prostate cancer combined.

Frank was reluctant to give me the results of his research because he knows I am not happy about my living situation. He said he didn't want to fuel the fire of my despondency. Give it to me, I told him. The good, bad, and ugly.

He circled a quote from an article on the Alzheimer's Association of Texas in a touching attempt to end his report on a high note. "... Alzheimer's disease/dementia is not a death sentence. Life doesn't end at diagnosis. People want and can still live their lives and contribute to something."

I'm losing my memory and other cognitive abilities, and that frightens me. At least now I know when I've had a fog, albeit after the fact. I'm headed toward a life with no past or future, only the present.

Dr. Kim and Sarah advise me to avoid stress. Well, whoever's writing notes in the daily crossword puzzle is jacking up my stress level. If it's a gag then I want to catch the jokester and put a stop to it. If it's real and someone is asking me for help, I need to learn who it is while I'm still capable of helping. While there's still time. Before the fog envelops me for good and my future diary pages are blank.

I miss Rebecca.

Chapter 8

Blackjack stared at Kenny as dinner was being served. Kenny asked if there was something on his mind.

"You've been busy, Puzzle Man. Word is, you've come out of your shell and turned into quite the friendly resident. What's that all about?"

Kenny leaned back and smiled. "I decided enough is enough. If the people I know best are at this table, then I need to upgrade my circle of friends. You're the exception, Maisey."

"Oh oh, Puzzle Man is getting feisty," said Frank. "I think there's hope for this guy after all."

The small-portions-meal was bland. Kenny automatically reached for the salt before realizing there was no shaker on the table. Never had been. Maisey cocked an eyebrow at Kenny and said something unintelligible. No doubt chastising him for even thinking about consuming salt.

Kenny removed a small notebook from his shirt pocket and flipped pages. He found what he was looking for: names and unit numbers of five rooms on the first floor. They were selected at random on one of his now frequent walks. Blackjack asked if Kenny had become a bookie and, if so, he wanted odds on the Houston Rockets' winning the NBA this coming basketball season.

"No, Blackjack, nothing close to it," said Kenny. "It's just a to-do list. My doc and daughter are on my case to keep track of what I eat, how much I exercise and other stuff."

Blackjack's expression turned serious. "Promise me that if *AARP Magazine* hears about your note taking and hires you to write an article about life at Gulf Breeze, you'll give me considerable mention. You know, handsome, articulate, popular, and humble."

Kenny stood and pushed in his chair. "I'll tell you what, Blackjack, if AARP does hire me, you will be part of the article. And I promise I'll only write the truth about you."

"The truth? On second thought, you can give my space to Frank."

Tomorrow would be a big day for Kenny. For the first time since moving to Gulf Breeze four months earlier, he had a mission beyond muddling through his predictable and mundane daily routine. He was going to play detective by knocking on the doors of neighbors and engaging in chit-chat to try to determine who was leaving the cry-for-help messages in the crossword puzzles. His approach would involve visiting rooms until he either identified the mystery puzzler, ran out of neighbors, or could no longer continue.

The conversations had to come across as friendly and low-key to avoid the perception of an ulterior motive. Oldsters could be a suspicious lot as he well knew. Frank had shown Kenny how to Google web sites dealing with police and military interrogation techniques. Carefully worded questions, mostly open-ended, were proven to be effective in eliciting desired responses, he had read.

The outside of each unit had a small, decorative sign with the name of the residents painted in swirly handwriting. His own sign read "Welcome! Kenny Boone Lives Here." He'd jot down residents' names and room numbers on each floor and then conduct two visits a day–one in the morning and the other in the afternoon. A daunting task for the reticent retired Air Force mechanic, he realized, but one that needed to be done.

Kenny reviewed his list of questions again to commit them to memory. After each visit, he planned to rush back to his room and document the main takeaways from the conversations, such as key words, expressions, and body language "tells" described in Internet articles. At last, he turned out the light for what was sure to be a night of restless sleep.

Diary: June 12

I really stepped out of my comfort zone with this mission. Knocking on doors with a smile on my face is not something I'd do under normal circumstances, but this isn't normal. This is a mystery that has a ticking clock and needs solving. Call it fate or dumb luck, I've been tagged as the man for the job.

After three weeks of meet-and-greets with those couples that let me into their rooms (two declined), I'm at a stopping point. It's time to recharge my batteries and analyze my notes. Yeah, I'm exhausted, but pleased with my efforts. I'd be very surprised if the person I'm looking for... the mystery puzzler... isn't one of the residents I recently sat three feet from in a nice-to-meet-you setting.

The task now is to narrow down the list of likely puzzler candidates. Actually, they're all "likely" candidates; what I need is a short list of most probable candidates. I owe it to myself to apply due diligence to the evaluation of my notes and what I recall from the personal visits. I'm fairly certain that the findings will lead me to the right person.

Side note: I'm not nearly the enigma I was before starting this mission. People I have never spoken to are greeting me by name. A few still use Puzzle Man, but the tide is shifting toward Kenny almost daily. Sarah and Dr. Kim should give me a gold star for my progress with socialization. Impressive, but I don't think Welcome Wagon will be hiring me anytime.

Frank and Blackjack are getting an earful from residents who are curious about my sudden transformation to a friendly, outgoing guy. Me? If they knew the real reason for my being neighborly, their perception of me would change. It might even frighten a few.

One thing I hadn't expected was the collateral damage brought about by the new Kenny. Okay, damage might be a harsh description. What I mean is that the flip-side to Kenny the Second is an obligation, a responsibility really, to not revert to my old ways. Where before I could walk around Gulf Breeze in a comfortable cocoon of anonymity, today is a different story. Residents are saying hello and smiling, which, I must admit, is kind of nice. I'm warming to the idea of being one of those good old boys I used to avoid.

Beats the hell out of continuous isolation and loneliness.

Chapter 9

"I can't believe what I'm hearing about you from Lucy," said Sarah. "You're making a fantastic turnaround. Do I dare say I told you so, Daddy?"

Kenny was happy that his daughter was happy. She'd been beating herself up since she moved him to Gulf Breeze six months ago. If Sarah thought he'd made a drastic turn toward accepting his new life, then he wasn't about to convince her otherwise.

"Things have changed for me, no doubt about it," said Kenny. "I don't know who's more surprised, the staff, residents, you or me. I wouldn't mind dialing back my celebrity status a bit... it's tiring to be friendly."

Sarah assured her father that she'd never known him to be unfriendly. Rather, he was reserved and private. Nothing to apologize about; on the contrary, she always respected his strong, silent type demeanor.

"Enjoy your new friends. They will help keep you young at heart," she predicted.

"Well, younger at heart is more like it. If being outgoing slowed down my fogs, I'd double my efforts. I don't see that happening. In fact, you know the frequency is increasing."

Kenny asked whether Dr. Kim had shared with her any further insights into his condition. He pleaded with Sarah not to sugarcoat the doctor's prognosis. He could take it.

"I would never be anything less than candid with you, Dad. You know everything I know about your Alzheimer's disease/dementia. Nothing's changed in Dr. Kim's forecast. Your AD is steadily progressing or declining, depending how you look at it. You feel okay?"

"Still scared, not knowing when my next fog will occur," said Kenny. "And wondering when I'll have a memory lapse that is permanent. How long will I live in La La Land?"

Sarah and Kenny sat in silence until she jumped up and retrieved a box by the door. She handed it to her father who raised his eyebrows while examining the box.

"Well, aren't you going to open it? It's from Justin. Here, this came separately."

Kenny noted the return address of College Station, Texas, but that locale didn't immediately register. Then it came to him: his grandson, Justin, was a junior at Texas A&M University. He was an engineering major who belonged to the Corps of Cadets, the largest uniformed organization of students in the nation.

"This is a pleasant surprise," said Kenny. "I haven't seen J-Man for a while. How's he doing in Aggieland?"

"He is doing fine, busy with summer semester midterms and Corps activities," said Sarah. "He always asks about you and wants me to be sure and tell you he'll be down to see you next chance he gets."

Kenny was fond of Justin, his daughter's only child. When Sarah and Nathan split and Nathan moved to Seattle,

Kenny stepped up his role as male role model. He talked with him at length about serving in the military–active duty or reserves. Justin hadn't yet decided if a career in the service was in his future, but his options were open.

The box contained two books and a cap. One book was about military aircraft from World War II to present; the other contained 300 large-print crossword puzzles. Both would keep Kenny occupied for months to come. The cap was dark blue and was embroidered with *US Air Force Vet* along with the American flag. He put on the cap and smiled.

"That was nice of Justin," said Kenny. "He's a good boy or man I should say. Now that I've gotten better on the computer, I'll surprise him with a thank-you e-mail. What do you think of that?"

"It would make his day," said Sarah. "Now, back to you. I have to tell you that I'm very happy that you're reaching out to neighbors. What got into you?"

Kenny was tempted to tell Sarah the truth, that the impetus for his change in behavior was to track down the mystery puzzler. He dismissed that thought, though, because he didn't want to dampen her high spirits. Let her think he'd turned the corner on his living arrangement while he covertly carried out his mission.

"Guess I got bored holing up with only my crossword puzzles for company," said Kenny. "I felt it was time to shake things up, keep my mind and body more active. You know, following doctor's orders."

Sarah gathered her purse and gave Kenny a hug before leaving. He said goodbye and stretched out on his recliner for a much-needed nap. When he awoke, he was going to review the notes from his visits with neighbors.

Kenny had recently narrowed the list of mystery puzzler suspects to four couples and one single man. He'd observed that in couple relationships one partner usually was in poorer health than the other partner, who by default was the live-in caretaker. Watching a partner linger or slip away could be overwhelming as Kenny knew from personal experience. Asking for help, even by way of a cryptic message left in a puzzle, was understandable. As for the single man, he struck Kenny as desperately unhappy and resentful... just like Kenny when he moved to Gulf Breeze.

Chapter 10

Walter and Carol – Glass is Half-Full (Room 177)

Kenny didn't know if Walter and Carol were born optimistic or came by it through a religious awakening. Regardless, they were a cheerful pair.

He recalled Walter's reaction when he knocked on their door. "Come on in. Here, take my comfy chair. We don't get many visitors. What can I do for you?" Walter was downright effusive. Carol seemed cautious and skeptical. She said she'd seen him working crossword puzzles in the game room, which was a hobby she used to enjoy until macular degeneration, an incurable condition, changed things. Blurred vision put a stop to that activity.

Kenny made a mental note about Carol being a crossword puzzle fan, then got right to the point of his visit. He restated his name and room number, assuming they probably didn't catch it the first time.

"I'm fairly new at Gulf Breeze," he said. "I never realized when I moved here how lonely it can be living in the same building with 150 other people of my vintage. Anyway, I decided to make an effort to get to know my neighbors. People like you."

Carol remarked that it wasn't unusual for new residents, particularly men, to think they could handle the isolation just fine. Some do, she pointed out, while others sink into depression. Loneliness will suck the life out of you if you let it, she pointed out. That was Walter's condition until he became a born-again friendly guy like he used to be as a younger man.

"Carol's right as always," Walter chuckled. "I was one sad old man… all I wanted to do was sleep and watch television. Carol was, and is, my rock. Before you think I'm a mental case, I do have neck and back pain something fierce. Most days I can barely put on shoes. Pain is a common contributor to depression."

Kenny listened to Walter, but his attention was drawn to Carol. There was a look about her that he found intriguing. She politely listened to her husband and nodded at the appropriate times. Yet, she seemed preoccupied. Kenny sensed there was something going on with her that didn't jibe with her pleasant expression.

"Carol, I have a feeling you're a big part of Walter's rebound," said Kenny. "My late wife pulled me along when I was at a low point after retiring from the Air Force. I didn't realize it at the time but taking care of me took a toll on her. I wasn't aware of the extent of her condition until it was too late. By the time she went to hospice, it was pretty much over."

"I'm okay, don't worry about me," she said. "Focusing on Walter is my job. A job I love and am happy to do."

Walter smiled and assured Kenny that they've had their share of ups and downs.

"We decided to stop dwelling on the negative and embrace the positive," said Walter. "It's amazing what a difference that kind of outlook makes on getting through each day."

Kenny took that as his cue to leave. He thanked them for their time and returned to his room to write down his impressions of Walter and Carol. His initial assessment was mixed: Walter appeared to be on somewhat shaky ground regarding his depression, maybe an episode or so away from relapsing. A downturn in Carol's health could push Walter back to despair.

Carol was an interesting person, Kenny observed. She put up a good front and said all the right things; however, Kenny believed there was turmoil and angst just under the surface. The strain of being her husband's cheerleader as well as coping with macular degeneration might be taking their toll. Was she suppressing a cry for help?Kenny realized he'd need to call on every bit of intuition, behavioral skills, and gut instincts he honed in the military to properly assess the nine residents. If Walter and Carol were typical, then he had his work cut out.

For now, Carol was the leading candidate for mystery puzzler.

Chapter 11

Blackjack and Frank were adamant. They'd been after Kenny for weeks to accompany them and Maisey to the local mall via the Gulf Breeze courtesy van. He finally agreed and was waiting for them in the lobby precisely at ten a.m. The timing was critical as he was compelled to work the crossword puzzle after checking it for new messages before doing anything else each day.

"Lookee here. Puzzle Man graces us with his presence," bellowed Blackjack. Frank was less obnoxious. He told Kenny to pay no mind to Blackjack. Not being a veteran, he said Blackjack should be indebted to them for providing personal security to him and Maisey.

"Hah," said Blackjack. "Like I need you two to protect us from the geriatric fitness walkers and millennial mall rats."

Kenny suggested they climb aboard the shuttle ahead of the others. He offered to help with Maisey and her wheelchair, but Blackjack assured him it was a one-man job.

The ride to Galveston Mall took about fifteen minutes. Blackjack chatted about this and that while Kenny and Frank were content to stare out the windows. Kenny was deep in thought about the next couple to visit, Bert and Yvonne, and didn't react when Blackjack repeatedly asked him a question. Kenny finally *heard* Blackjack, and his table mate was exasperated.

"Man, you keep zoning out like this and you may never come back," he admonished Kenny. "Maybe you should get hearing aids like the rest of us. Stop being in denial."

Kenny didn't see what the big deal was all about. He always could be laser focused when it mattered. That was one of his strong characteristics when he supervised aircraft mechanics. Identify the problem and fix it... period.

The residents shuffled into the mall with their assortment of wheelchairs, walkers, and canes. Kenny stuck with Blackjack, Maisey and Frank long enough to be polite, then peeled off in search of a hobby store. Crossword puzzles were still the recreational king, in his mind, yet he needed more to do. He needed something to balance the intensity of sleuthing for the mystery puzzler.

Kenny found a Hobby Lobby and began a slow inspection of its offerings. He considered stamp and coin collecting kits, chemistry set, classic car models, painting by numbers, and on and on. His head was swimming and he was on his way out of the store when his eye caught a display of interest. It was an assortment of drone airplanes–unmanned aerial vehicles–in various size and price selections.

A clerk saw Kenny ogling the drones and offered his assistance, which Kenny gladly accepted. Although a long-time Air Force aircraft mechanic, he always longed to be a pilot. Twice he took the tests to get admitted to flight school, but a minor case of color blindness kept him from his dream. With a drone, though, he could at last become a pilot.

Kenny listened intently as the clerk described available features of the drones such as a digital camera, smart phone controller, GPS, Wi-Fi enabled, and obstacle avoidance sensors. He handed Kenny a drone he said was a top seller. It was considered a mini-drone, had a 16-minute flight time, top speed of 30 miles per hour, and a maximum operating range of 100 meters. Price tag for this one was 399 dollars.

"I like it, but..." said Kenny. "I'm hesitant because I'm not a high-tech guy when it comes to the digital age. Is there a Drones for Dummies manual that comes with it?"

The clerk laughed and assured Kenny not to be overly concerned. He showed Kenny a quick-start guide that graphically explained all Kenny needed to know about operating the drone.

"I'll take it," said Kenny, telling himself Frank could be his personal IT guy if the drone controls proved to be too difficult. He paid for the purchase and walked out of the store in search of the food court.

He never made it.

Chapter 12

Sarah had left work in a rush. The text message was terse: "Incident with your father. He is fine. Come to Gulf Breeze."

Lucy met Sarah at the entrance and escorted her to the conference room. Dr. Kim was already seated with her laptop computer open and on. She gave Sarah a tense smile and gestured for Sarah to sit next to her.

"What's going on? Where's my father?"

Dr. Kim spoke. "He is sleeping peacefully in his room. I gave him a mild sedative. Mr. Boone is fine, physically. No injuries. Lucy, please tell Sarah what happened today."

Lucy cleared her throat. "As Dr. Kim said, your father is fine. He had another memory lapse. This time at Galveston Mall."

She went on to relate how Kenny had made a purchase at a hobby store and from there ended up in the women's shoe department of Macy's.

"Don't ask me how that happened," said Lucy. "Apparently, he told the Macy's people that he was waiting for his wife, who was shopping elsewhere in the store. They left him alone to wait... for two hours."

"In the meantime," Lucy continued, "the shuttle was ready to return to Gulf Breeze. The driver did a headcount and came up one rider short. Mall security was alerted and the first sweep did not locate your father. Announcements were made on the loudspeaker and a sharp clerk made the connection. She called security and voila!"

Dr. Kim said Kenny was evaluated by an EMT at the mall and cleared to ride back to Gulf Breeze in the shuttle. When Dr. Kim arrived, she administered the sedative to Kenny who was resting in his room. Lucy arranged for a nurse to check on him every thirty minutes.

Sarah's head was lowered, and she spoke softly. "My mother died years ago. He said he was waiting for her. Oh my God, that's so sad."

"His delusion is consistent with dementia," said Dr. Kim. "The 'fogs' as he calls them, often are just periods when he has no idea what's going on around him. In this latest case, his mind resurrected a very strong, deep-rooted memory. Your late mother."

Sarah asked if this was the way it was going to continue, more fogs and delusional episodes. All leading to where?

Dr. Kim recommended that Kenny be admitted to the memory care unit of Gulf Breeze. This involved 24-hour supervised care by a skilled nursing staff trained in helping people with Alzheimer's, dementia and other types of memory challenges. For example, if Kenny wanted to take another excursion to the mall, he'd be accompanied by one of the nurses who'd monitor his behavior.

When Sarah started to get agitated, Lucy held up her hand and said her father could continue to reside in his room and avail himself of all Gulf Breeze amenities. The only significant change would be his level of care. Sarah took a deep breath and let herself relax.

"When would this begin?" Sarah wondered.

"Dr. Kim has already signed off on his move to memory care," said Lucy. With your agreement, the change in status will begin the moment he awakes."

Sarah thanked them for their help and apologized for the trouble her father caused today. She excused herself and went to room 258 where her father was talking in his sleep. Sarah could only distinguish the words 'help' and 'puzzle'. She held his hand and worried.

Diary: July 1

So, it happened again. This time the fog was in a women's shoe section of a large department store? Unbelievable. They say I spent two hours waiting for my wife. I know she's gone... I think about Rebecca every day. I am grateful that Blackjack hasn't ribbed me about that episode. I need to stay on his good side to avoid getting teased. Frank is cool about it. He wouldn't embarrass a fellow vet.

Boy was I surprised to wake up and see a drone airplane on the bedside table. In a few minutes it came back to me: shuttle to the mall, hobby store, drone purchase and then... nothing. Back in my room with a nurse hovering over me.

She said Sarah had just left and would be back later in the day.

Lucy had come by, too, and briefly explained memory care. She left a brochure that went into detail about how memory care meant a more structured environment with set schedules and routines to create a stress-free lifestyle. They are big on stress, or lack of it, around here. I still have to interview four additional couples and check the daily crosswords so stress-free will have to wait.

Memory care is big on enhanced safety features, whatever that all entails. Perhaps I'll need a nurse to accompany me into the bathroom. Do I get to pick that particular nurse? And there will be additional programs to enhance my cognitive skills. Bingo here I come.

I shouldn't complain although as a career NCO that's what I do. My declining condition is dictating the level of care. Sarah, Dr. Kim, and Lucy are on top of things. I know Sarah won't let them do anything drastic to me unless absolutely necessary. Visions of Jack Nicholson as Randall McMurphy in One Flew Over the Cuckoo's Nest comes to mind. The electroconvulsive therapy he received was nasty stuff. I wonder if my Air Force medical coverage would pay for that kind of therapy or at least a rubber room. Ah, there I go again. I should try to be more like Walter.

Starting tomorrow I'm getting back to my routine with the daily crossword puzzle, breakfast with Blackjack, Maisey, and Frank, and then my next round of interviews. After an afternoon siesta I'll get to work on the drone. Captain Kenny is waiting to fly.

Fourth of July is a few days away. It's always been a favorite holiday of mine. Wish I could get in a time machine and light fireworks with Rebecca and Sarah just one more time.

Chapter 13

Bert and Yvonne – God's Will (Room 309)

Kenny's visit with Bert and Yvonne was brief, but productive. Kenny wouldn't have been surprised to hear the song "Que Sera, Sera" sung by Doris Day playing in the background. The couple appeared laid-back and content with the status quo.

"You know how the elderly like to talk about their afflictions? That's us," said Yvonne, a spry 90-year-old. "I have rheumatoid arthritis; Bert here has diabetes and so many plastic parts in his body I call him Mr. Potato Head."

"You crack me up, dear," said Bert. "Now why don't you take your comedy routine into the kitchen and get us a snack."

When she returned with a cheese log and platter of crackers, she explained that years ago she and Bert came to grips with their conditions and chose not to make it the focal point of their elderly lives.

"Basically, we don't complain," said Bert with a nervous laugh. "Being negative is no way to live. You probably know by now, Kenny, who the whiners are at Gulf Breeze. I don't see you as one of those, so we're happy to get to know you."

Kenny didn't bother to correct Bert on his opinion of him as a non-whiner.

They talked about careers and families until Kenny could feel the energy in the room waning. He took a risk with his new friends by shifting gears and asking pointed questions about life in a senior living facility generally, and Gulf Breeze specifically.

Bert and Yvonne maintained their go-with-the-flow attitude, repeatedly citing God's will as the roadmap for their senior years. Yvonne elaborated by telling Kenny that God has a divine plan for everyone, so why fight fate? Bert echoed Yvonne's statements, and added that he believed worry and stress are as dangerous as a disease.

"Yeah, I've been hearing a lot about my stress level since moving here," said Kenny, "My daughter and doctor are always harping on me to relax and do things like meditation. You two do that?

Yvonne grinned and said they used to. "Not anymore because it just didn't seem real. We're realists, Kenny, we take things as they come and don't sweat the small stuff. Especially Bert. You ought to try it, it'll make life easier."

Kenny sat back and assessed the dynamics of Bert and Yvonne. He wasn't convinced that all was as the couple had proclaimed. Yvonne's eyes shot daggers at Bert when he made an offhand remark suggesting that with divine will in play, what's the point in bucking the inevitable, good or bad? Yvonne shook her head slightly, as if to tell Bert not to go there.

How'd that song go? *Whatever will be, will be. The future's not ours to see, que sera, sera.*

Kenny had his doubts. Mr. Potato Head talked a good game, but Kenny's gut told him that the man didn't totally buy into the God's will philosophy. Bert now was on the mystery puzzler list with Carol.

Chapter 14

Kenny and Frank were becoming buddies beyond the meals they shared with Blackjack and Maisey. Since the mall episode, Frank regularly asked Kenny how he was doing, and occasionally knocked on Kenny's door during the day. Frank always had something in mind, like going for a walk, showing Kenny a new computer application, or an invitation to take cups of coffee into the courtyard when the weather was comfortable. Kenny appreciated that Frank was looking after him.

Lately, though, Kenny was tracking down Frank to get help with his drone model airplane. The nuances of mastering the controls were a challenge for Kenny. Frank had experience with his grandchildren's video games and knew enough about computer applications to get Kenny proficient in operating his plane, albeit not without a few gentle crash landings.

Kenny's extensive experience repairing military aircraft came into play with minor modifications he made to the drone's landing gear and wing configuration. He couldn't help himself, he told Frank, who was impressed with Kenny's keen eye for detail.

"You've forgotten more about airplanes than I'll ever know," said Frank. "But you are behind the times when it comes to joining the computer age. Don't worry, I'll teach you as long as I get to fly the plane."

"That's a deal I can live with," said Kenny. "In fact, let's go to the vacant lot across the street this afternoon for flight practice. The drone's battery will be fully charged by then."

The new rules of Kenny's memory care status required that he be accompanied by a nurse's aide whenever he left Gulf Breeze, unless he was with Sarah or Dr. Kim. This meant making arrangements through Lucy in advance. Kenny was miffed that something as simple as walking to the adjacent lot to fly the drone generated a paper trail. Apparently, Frank didn't qualify as a suitable chaperone, a fact that Blackjack found humorous.

"I could babysit you two if I wasn't already so busy with other commitments," said Blackjack at lunch. "Let's see, I'm polishing my dress shoes, cleaning out our mini-fridge, entering Publishers Clearinghouse, and taking Maisey to the manicurist."

"Yeah, yeah I get it," said Kenny. "Your services are in big demand. Frank and I would be honored if one day you could juggle your schedule and go with us to fly the drone. Maisey, too."

Blackjack had no snappy retort to Kenny's offer. He shrugged and finished his sandwich. Kenny advised Frank that a nurse's aide was available from two to three that afternoon. They'd meet in the lobby and walk over together.

Kenny was getting the hang of flying the drone thanks to Frank's patient instruction. Manipulating the controller was intuitive once he got comfortable with its basic operation. Frank was less adept because he wasn't familiar with the concept of lift and its relationship to moving the plane upward by way of forward motion. As a team, however, they complemented each other and improved rapidly.

The nurse's aide was amused watching the two old men fly the plane, Kenny observed. When he offered her a turn she politely declined, citing she was "on duty."

"You guys certainly are enjoying yourselves," she said. "It's good to see you out in the fresh air having fun. Great therapy."

They didn't need the one hour time allotted for the outing as the drone's battery was drained after only a half hour. They killed some of the remaining minutes by walking around the lot and noting the cloud formations, which was something neither had done for years. Frank said that flying the drone gave him a new appreciation for how beautiful the sky was on a sunny day.

"I'm going to get on Amazon and buy a second battery," said Kenny on the walk back to Gulf Breeze. "If we only get an hour, we might as well use it flying. After all, I'm a pilot now."

Frank looked at Kenny and said he guessed that made him Kenny's wingman.

"Talk to me, Goose," Kenny said, quoting a line from *Top Gun*.

"Goose? I'm a waterfowl? Time for your nap, Kenny."

Chapter 15

Herb and Barbara – Glass is Half-Empty (Room 138)

Kenny vividly recalled this visit. He was kept waiting in the hallway for several minutes and overheard muted arguing and shushing between a man and woman. When they finally came to the door both appeared flushed and rattled.

It was obvious that Kenny had come at an awkward moment for the couple. He offered to return another time, but they insisted he come in and make himself comfortable. He came in yet comfort was difficult with so much tension in the air.

"Look, it would be no problem for me to come back another time," said Kenny. "It just so happens my schedule is free for... the rest of my life."

Barbara, a tiny woman with a big voice, said the racket he probably heard from the hallway was an old movie on TV. They had the volume cranked high because they both were hard of hearing.

Kenny almost commented that the two characters on TV sounded exactly like Herb and Barbara. He let it pass. They were flustered and didn't need Kenny to be judgmental right off the bat.

Their story was typical of so many others at Gulf Breeze: Married 60-plus years, adult children and grandchildren scattered throughout the U.S., siblings in assisted-living homes in the Southwest, they no longer drove or flew, each had medical issues, and the list went on. Kenny felt right at home.

What differentiated them from most other residents he'd met was that Herb and Barbara didn't even try to put a positive spin on things. In fact, they pointed out all that was wrong with little effort to express gratitude for what should be bringing them happiness: each other, family, friends, a comfortable place to live with amenities, and generally good health for the age. Arthritis, diminished hearing, and Herb's pacemaker for his irregular heartbeat seemed to be the extent of their health concerns. So, Kenny wondered, why so glum?

Barbara, who was the spokesperson for the couple, must have read Kenny's mind.

"You consider yourself a lucky man?" she said to Kenny and then continued before he could reply. "Well, in our case, if we didn't have bad luck, we wouldn't have any luck at all. That's just the way it is for us, always has been."

Kenny made the point that their lives must be filled with smart choices and favorable outcomes. Herb shook his head vigorously.

"Let me lay it out for you. We couldn't have kids; I had a dead-end career and for some reason people don't warm up to me. That sound like any kind of life to you?"

Barbara jumped in again by launching another question Kenny's way. She asked what he thought of a husband who blamed his wife for being unable to have children and held a grudge for decades. She quickly added, "Never mind, I don't want to know."

It wasn't Kenny's place to enable their pessimism. Instead, he moved the conversation to hobbies. He described his recent acquisition of a drone aircraft and his life-long addiction to crossword puzzles. He watched for any reaction to "puzzle" from Herb or Barbara. Only a slight facial tic from Herb.

When they got into a spat over what time to go down for dinner, Kenny made his getaway. Strange couple, he mused. Not sure if none or both make the mystery puzzler list. Back in his room he wrote "unsure - possible" next to their names.

Chapter 16

The dining room was ablaze with red, white, and blue decorations. Fourth of July had arrived, and Gulf Breeze had gone all out to acknowledge the holiday in a big way. Kenny stopped in his tracks when he went to breakfast and soon after about choked on his toast when he saw Lucy dressed in clothing of the colonial period.

"Isn't this something?" said Blackjack, his arm around Maisey's shoulders. "Makes me proud to be a black American."

Maisey pushed her husband's arm away and glared. Blackjack explained that she didn't approve of him referring to himself as a "black" American, seeing how she was white, and they were married.

"She's right," said Frank. "We're all Americans. All different colors, religions, and beliefs. That makes us a strong country even with the divisiveness among some individuals and groups."

Kenny was impressed with Frank's analysis of the state of America today. The one-time Marine was as solid as they came and was getting to be Kenny's closest friend at Gulf Breeze. The military veteran bond they shared had a lot to do with their growing camaraderie.

Lucy stopped by their table and invited them to participate in the special activities planned for the day and evening, culminating with a firework show on the back lawn. She said the July 4 schedule of events was posted throughout the building.

"Mr. Boone, are you good enough with your drone plane to put on an exhibition for your neighbors? Perhaps after dinner for about ten minutes out where the fireworks will take place?"

Kenny and Frank looked at each other at the same time. They nodded and Kenny told Lucy it would cost her an extra dessert for his table. She laughed and asked why the entire table since only he and Frank fly the plane.

"I am the pilot, Frank is my wingman, and Blackjack and Maisey are ground crew. We're a team."

Blackjack gave Kenny an admiring look. "Yeah," he said. "Like Puzzle Man says, we're a team, Team 14. You know, our table number."

Lucy had revised the schedule of events to include "Drone plane demonstration by Kenny Boone and his flight crew." The folding chairs out on the lawn began filling up early. Kenny assumed that the upcoming fireworks was the main attraction and he was fine with that. He and Frank had worked out the details of their show and were confident that the ten minutes they were allotted would be both entertaining and educational.

Kenny was telling the small gathering about the plane and its capabilities when one of the spectators yelled out.

"Come on, Puzzle Man, we don't need a history lesson. Fly the damn thing."

Kenny cut his opening remarks and launched the drone. He demonstrated liftoff, hovering, flying in a circle, flying left, right, forward, and backward, and landing. At the end of the demo he took the plane up about one hundred feet and directed it downward toward the seated audience. He zeroed in on the man who had interrupted his presentation and then made the plane rise sharply, fly in a lazy arc, and land softly on the lawn.

"Geez, Kenny," said Frank as he helped stow the plane. "Did you consider that any one of them could have had a heart attack when you flew right at them. I almost had one–I didn't know you could fly like that."

Kenny's smile said it all. "It was a risk, I'll admit it. But did you see the look on the face of that loudmouth guy? It was beautiful."

"I didn't disapprove of you buzzing the crowd," said Frank. "I actually enjoyed the heck out of it. Sorry I missed the guy's expression when the plane dove at him. Must have been priceless."

Kenny's smile got even bigger. "It was priceless. You can see it for yourself. I had the camera on during the dive. That footage will become a legend at Gulf Breeze."

Chapter 17

Sarah was struggling with her emotions. She knew in her heart that moving Dad to a senior living home was the right course of action considering his declining condition, yet she couldn't forgive herself or dismiss the guilt for going about her life while he was being cared for by others.

Sarah visited him regularly, consulted with Dr. Lee and Lucy often, and had accumulated a small library of reference materials covering Alzheimer's disease and dementia. She'd even joined a support group for family members of AD/D relatives. If there was any adult offspring fully on board with trying to do what's best for an ailing parent, it was Sarah. Still...

At a recent support group meeting, Sarah sat next to a woman whose mother was in a memory care unit a few miles from Gulf Breeze. They struck up a conversation waiting for the meeting to begin and by the end of the night had exchanged e-mail addresses.

"Hi, I'm Kay. I've seen you here a couple of times. You new to the group?"

"Pretty new, yes. My name is Sarah. How long have you attended these meetings?"

Kay said it'd been two years. Her mother's condition was stable, meaning no significant changes for months. Sarah explained that her father's condition was in flux– good days mostly, with bad days sprinkled in. She told Kay about his "fogs" and increasing memory lapses.

"Sounds familiar," said Kay. "My mother is child-like these days. She likes to look at family photo albums and watch cartoons on television. Some days she doesn't know who I am."

"Oh, I'm so sorry. I can't imagine how you handle not being recognized by your mother. It would be devastating if my father asked who I was."

"It could happen so don't be shocked if it does," said Kay. "Forgetfulness and regression are common traits of dementia. I tell myself that deep inside my mother knows it's me. She's changed... still changing... and I'm the one who has to adapt."

Sarah went home with a lot on her mind. Kay might have just become her new best friend. Kenny was changing and it was beyond his control or comprehension. She must adapt, as Kay had, and be there for her father no matter who he was becoming. New Kennys required new Sarahs.

Sarah's mobile phone rang while she was at work. The caller ID said Gulf Breeze. This couldn't be good, she thought, excusing herself from a staff meeting to take the call.

"Sarah? It's Lucy. Your father is fine so don't be too alarmed. He did have an episode I wanted to tell you about. He went to his room after dinner and locked the door. He also wedged a book under the door. When the nurse's aide came to give him his meds in the morning, she knocked and there was no answer. She unlocked the door, but the book kept her from entering.

"Bottom line is one of our maintenance guys had to remove the door so we could get inside. Mr. Boone was in his recliner and slightly delirious. He'd wet himself and was unaware of his situation. We cleaned him up, gave him liquids and a sedative, and put him in bed. Dr. Kim has been notified."

Sarah left work early and rushed to Gulf Breeze. Her father was sitting up in bed with a crossword puzzle book open and pencil in hand.

"Hi, sweetheart. I didn't expect a visit from you today. This is a nice surprise."

Sarah took his hand and asked how he was doing. She noted the puzzlement on his face and thought about how Kay's mother had changed due to dementia. Her father didn't remember locking and wedging the door or the rest of the previous eighteen hours.

"I was at work and decided I'd rather be with you," said Sarah. "You look well rested. What do you have planned for this afternoon?"

Kenny gazed out the window. "I was thinking of driving my pickup to Johnson Space Center. It's been a while since I visited the space museum. Want to come along?"

"I have another idea. Why don't I take you to lunch and then you fly your drone plane for me? I hear you're a really good pilot. No surprise... Air Force veteran."

"That's a fine idea. Besides, I can't find my keys and I forgot where I parked my truck."

Sarah said she'd meet him in the lobby when he was ready to go. She decided not to remind her father that she took away his truck keys more than six months ago.

Chapter 18

Stan and Margaret – One Day at a Time (Room 420)

Similar to Bert and Yvonne, this couple followed the mantra of accepting whatever life circumstances came their way. It struck Kenny as odd that both individuals in a long-term relationship had the same state of mind. A coincidence or perhaps one partner had converted to keep peace in the marriage. He and Rebecca were opposites on many things, which made for a lively, sometimes contentious, and always stimulating sixty-plus years.

"We like it here at Gulf Breeze. It was our first choice once we realized that navigating stairs in our two-story home was not a long-term prospect," said Stan, a tall drink of water with a protruding Adam's apple. As he spoke, Margaret nodded her head, as he did when she spoke.

Margaret clarified her husband's comment by pointing out that he took a tumble on the stairway, badly wrenching his knee and requiring him to sleep on the family room couch for four weeks. Right on cue he nodded.

"No big deal," he continued. "The couch was comfortable, and I got to watch my sports shows when she went to bed. Oh, did I mention being close to the kitchen?"

Kenny soon got the message loud and clear: you can't control what happens all the time so relax and enjoy the ride. Further discussion with them touched on health (not bad), physical limitations (creaky joints), social life (not much), hobbies (TV), family (a son in Oregon and daughter in Washington state), religion (overrated), and their expectations for what's to come as they age (if there is a God, please make the end quick and painless). Kenny worked in a question about keeping their minds nimble via activities like crossword puzzles. They hesitated briefly and Margaret shook her head this time. Stan followed her lead.

In all subjects they covered with Kenny, the couple seemed unfazed by an uncertain future with potential roadblocks.

"Some days I wouldn't mind if a massive heart attack took me out," said Stan. "I mean death is inevitable, right? Do I sound crazy?"

"I think you sound realistic," said Margaret. "We're not exactly living like the Trump family. We know what to expect as the years tick by. Look around, this place is one big geriatric waiting room. Is it worth it?"

Kenny wasn't sure if he was being played by the couple. They might get their kicks shocking people with their "ending it all" sentiments. On the other hand, if there was even a hint of truth to what they were saying, harming themselves or each other couldn't be ruled out.

Stan and Margaret were strange and a little scary, Kenny surmised. Because of their outlandish remarks he put them near the top of his mystery puzzler list.

He'd have two glasses of wine before dinner tonight.

Chapter 19

The mystery puzzler struck again. This time the message within the puzzle was *getting late.* He had to hand it to the person, he or she was good at aligning columns and rows to form intersecting words. Kenny wondered for the gazillionth time, *Who are you? Why don't you step forward and get the help you seem to so desperately need?*

Of course, there was never a reply. It was up to him to crack the mystery puzzler case in his own way. He still had the single man to visit, then he'd be done with his top five list of four couples and the single man. Kenny wasn't sure where he'd go from there. There were several likely candidates so far; how to cull that short list was something he hadn't spent much time mulling over. That would come in the near future.

"Hey Kenny, we going to fly today?" Frank had followed Kenny from the dining room to the game room. He was scanning the sports section while Kenny worked the crossword.

Kenny set down his pencil. Ordinarily he'd be perturbed at the interruption. Residents had learned to give Puzzle Man privacy when he was at the table with the daily newspaper spread out before him. Frank, though, was another story. The two had become fast friends.

"Sure thing. I'll put in a request for a nurse's aide and see if one is available," said Kenny. "I need you to help me figure out how to finesse the controller to have the plane do a loop maneuver. I'm afraid if I do it on my own, it'll crash."

Frank agreed and headed to the computer room to research Kenny's request. He said a good place for him to begin was the chat room of a drone aircraft hobbyist web site he discovered. Anything you wanted to know about building, flying, customizing, or repairing a drone was accessible on that web site. Frank told Kenny he was well on his way to becoming a "drone nerd."

Kenny picked up his pencil and got back to work on the puzzle when a second visitor approached him that morning. Lucy was making her rounds and sat across from Kenny at the table.

"I see you're back to your morning routine after recovering from your latest episode," she said. "How're you feeling today, Mr. Boone?"

"Still a little groggy and slow-moving, but steadily improving. It bothers me that there is no prior warning when I have one of my fogs... all I know is I wake up and am told after the fact what happened. It frightens me."

Lucy reminded Kenny that his safety and comfort were the top priorities of Gulf Breeze, and that he was in good hands. The upgrade in his status to memory care meant increased attention from the staff and ongoing analyses of his behavior.

"We're here for you, Mr. Boone. So are your daughter and Dr. Kim. You are not alone with your dementia even though you may feel that way. However, you can't be locking your door and wedging a book beneath it. That caused a bit of a stir."

Kenny looked chagrined. "I don't even remember doing that," he said.

Lucy wished Kenny a good day and resumed her rounds. His interest in today's puzzle had waned. As he rose his eyes locked on the mystery puzzler's latest message. Kenny told himself to finish his visits with the top five and put an end to the mystery.

Chapter 20

Russell – Solitary Man (Room 223)

It was like looking into a mirror. Kenny had no brothers, but a brother from another mother? He thought that Russell might be that person.

Russell also was a widower who lived alone. He had chronic obstructive pulmonary disease (COPD) and used an oxygen system several hours a day to help his breathing. His son had moved Russell to Gulf Breeze after two weeks in a hospital. Like Kenny, Russell retired after more than thirty years with the same organization. Unlike Kenny, it wasn't the military. He was a middle manager at a major oil company until yet another corporate reorganization prompted him to hang it up.

"I've seen you around and until now you've just been another geezer at Gulf Breeze," said Russell. "A little out of the ordinary to come calling. I'm as straight as they come, in case you're wondering."

"Whoa, hold on," Kenny blurted. "Where'd that come from? I'm just a guy who's trying to meet his neighbors and make a few new friends. That's all."

With the opening round out of the way, the two men got along rather well. Kenny had finally met someone who shared the same wry humor as him, including well-timed wisecracks and light sarcasm. They were on the same wavelength, Kenny could tell, with one important exception: Russell had not yet

77

come to terms with his life in a senior living facility and fought it at every turn.

Russell reminded Kenny of how he was when Sarah moved him to Gulf Breeze. Lonely, alone, frustrated, and in denial. Kenny had mellowed in those areas, but Russell was far from accepting the status quo.

"I'm telling you, Kenny, that if my son hadn't talked me into selling my home, I'd be in it right now," said Russell. "I'd climb out the window and run away if I had a place to go. This place is fine, I have no complaints other than being here. I want to go home."

Kenny was taken aback because he'd felt the same way only a few months ago. The memories rushed back at him in emotional waves. Russell noticed his reaction and asked if Kenny could use a soft drink or beer. Kenny raised his hand while he collected himself.

"I'm okay, had a deja vu experience listening to you," said Kenny. "This may sound funny, but you sound an awful lot like I did when my daughter moved me here. I like to think I've moved on... now I'm not so sure."

Russell grabbed two beers from the fridge and brought them into the living room. He handed one to Kenny and took a swig from the other. Finally, Russel conceded, he met someone at Gulf Breeze who could relate to what he was going through.

"I envy how you've adapted," said Russell. "The odds of me 'moving on' are slim to none. I want to go home."

Kenny suggested that Russell pursue hobbies, reading, listening to music, anything to fill up the long days of living alone.

"I got myself a drone airplane at the mall and fly it a couple times a week. I also am a crossword puzzle addict. You ever do crosswords, Russell?"

Russell took another drink and said, "Yes, as a matter of fact, I enjoy crosswords and am pretty good at them, too. Why do you ask?"

"Oh, no particular reason," said Kenny. "Just making conversation."

They talked about sports for the next fifteen minutes, specifically the Astros, Rockets and Texans. Russell offered another beer, which Kenny declined.

"One beer is good for me as well," said Russell. "I don't want to get pulled over by a cop when I run errands today."

"You still drive?"

"Of course. I lost my home, but I'll never let go of my pickup truck. You don't drive? You seem capable to me."

Kenny sighed and explained how Sarah had taken his truck keys before he moved into Gulf Breeze. He left out the part about the Silver Alert. Kenny didn't want to burden Russell with a description of his memory lapses, so he told him his daughter didn't think he needed a vehicle any longer. He got rides with family or took the shuttle. Kenny also failed to mention that he had to be accompanied by an approved chaperone in order to leave the premises.

"Tell you what, you need a ride you come see me," said Russell. "And if you want to drive once in a while, that can be arranged. This ain't a prison... we're still free men last time I checked."

Kenny returned to his room and stretched out on the recliner. His visit with Russell was a wake-up call that had stirred suppressed feelings. Maybe he hadn't moved on with his life as much as he implied to Russell. Kenny wondered if he was indeed happier since arriving at Gulf Breeze or simply playing a role to please Sarah?

Never mind my own situation for now, he told himself. What about Russell? He was an angry man whose sentiments matched Kenny's when he was a new resident. Kenny didn't think that Russell was the type to ask for help in a crossword puzzle considering how direct he came across in person. However, he liked puzzles, so...

Kenny figured Russell might be the type of person who enjoyed bitching and moaning out loud to anyone who would listen. Worst case he was an emotional time bomb waiting to go off. Or more likely he fell somewhere between the two extremes.

He put Russell at the bottom of the mystery puzzler suspects list–a placeholder for future evaluation.

Chapter 21

Sarah was both nervous and excited. After days of Kenny pleading to come home for a weekend, she, Lucy, and Dr. Kim had worked out the details to make this happen. The do's and don'ts list covered such things as medications, foods to forgo, stress avoidance, personal hygiene, safety, and security. Marked in red ink were *don't leave him alone in the house, hide the car keys, and set the alarm at night.*

They enjoyed a simple meal of chili and hot dogs on Friday evening. Kenny's appetite was good and he helped himself to a second hot dog. She said no to more chili per doctor's orders to limit spicy foods.

"That hit the spot. I don't get chili at Gulf Breeze," said Kenny. "Unless you want me to help clean up after dinner, I'm going to get reacquainted with my old friend the couch and turn on the Astros baseball game. They're playing the Cardinals."

Sarah assured him she could handle the kitchen duties and got busy clearing the table. She was loading the last of the bowls and utensils into the dishwasher when her mobile phone chirped. She glanced at the readout and saw it was her son, Justin.

"Hi, honey, glad you called," said Sarah. "Guess who's about twenty feet from me watching baseball on TV? Your grandfather is here for the weekend... Really? He'll be happy to hear that. See you tomorrow."

Sarah hit the television's mute button and gave Kenny the good news. Justin had a short break from summer school and was going to visit this weekend. He said he was excited to see his favorite grandpa.

"Terrific," said Kenny. "I miss J-Man. "We can go bowling or play miniature golf like in the old days. I saw my pickup truck in the garage. Is the battery charged?"

"Dad, stop and think. You no longer drive. Remember your Silver Alert? I do and it was traumatic."

"But Justin can drive, I'll ride shotgun. There, problem solved."

Sarah let her breath out slowly before replying, telling herself *stress avoidance.* "You agreed to obey the rules for the home visit. One of them is you must be accompanied by me or someone else who's been pre-approved. Justin is not on the list. You two can spend quality time around the house... no need to drive anywhere."

Kenny clearly didn't like the rules and grumbled about being what amounted to a prisoner of war. He wondered how Russell would react to such limitations. He probably wouldn't put up with the restrictions and do what he pleased, just like Kenny would have done before he was sentenced to Gulf Breeze.

"You hear me, Dad? You going to behave?"

"Yeah, yeah I heard you. I'll try not to violate parole."

Justin got a late start on Saturday from College Station, arriving in Galveston at dinner time. The three of them, in a split decision, voted to eat at a local barbecue joint. Afterward, they took a stroll along the sea wall and were treated to a spectacular sunset over the Gulf of Mexico.

"I never get tired of this view," said Kenny. "Sometimes I go to the top floor of Gulf Breeze and look out a hallway window at the sun setting. It's a good time to think about things."

"Gulf Breeze sounds like a really nice place," said Justin. "Reminds me of my college dormitory, but without the loud music and partying. How's the food?

Kenny described typical meals: small portions, bland, lots of fruits and vegetables, and sugar-free desserts. He explained how as you get older your appetite and ability to taste food lessen.

"For me, it's become eating to live rather than living to eat. That's a shame because you know how I like to eat, or used to. I still enjoy my coffee in the morning. The caffeine kick helps me push through the daily crossword puzzles."

"Mom tells me you've become quite the social butterfly," said Justin. "Have you made some good friends?"

"I mostly have made acquaintances. You know, people you see day after day that you nod at or say hello to. There is one man I consider a friend. His name is Frank and he's a retired Marine, although I've learned not to refer to him as 'retired.' He and I fly my drone airplane as often as we can."

Sarah mentioned that Lucy had told her how Kenny was trying to get to know his neighbors by knocking on doors and introducing himself. He was getting to be known as Kenny or Mr. Boone instead of the reclusive Puzzle Man.

"That's great, Grandpa, although I have to admit that I can't see you going door to door meeting people. You're not the welcome wagon type, no offense."

Kenny smiled and said no offense taken. "I spent the first few months at Gulf Breeze blaming others for my lifestyle change. I blamed my doctor for her diagnosis of my dementia, which led to the move to Gulf Breeze. I blamed your mother for deciding that I could no longer reside in her home. I also blamed myself."

Justin was bewildered. "How could you blame yourself? You're 84 for Pete's sake."

"My military career ingrained in me the belief that I could manage almost everything that came my way," said Kenny. "And I did just that until I began experiencing the fogs... memory lapses. I thought if I concentrated more on what I was doing I could ward off the fogs. It's not working."

Sarah said that Kenny took a personal risk by going outside his comfort zone. "He could have gotten the cold shoulder from the first person he approached and called it quits. I'm proud of you, Daddy."

There was no response from Kenny. He felt like an impostor accepting praise from his daughter and grandson when his Mr. Neighbor routine had nothing to do with making new friends. If it wasn't for the mystery puzzler's cries for help,

Kenny would still be cooped up in his room watching TV and moping. He didn't have the courage to tell his family the truth, and he wasn't sure why.

Sarah accurately read her father's changing mood and suggested they head back to the house. The two men could watch the Astros game while she kicked back with a book by her favorite author, Pat Conroy. She locked the doors, set the alarm, and bid them goodnight.

"Nobody's to leave the house until morning," said Sarah. "We're on lockdown until the sun rises."

Justin said he was in for the night, then asked where she thought they might go.

Kenny looked at his grandson and winked. "Anywhere, my boy, anywhere."

Diary: July 20

What the hell is wrong with me? Tossing and turning in bed, my mind racing, vivid dreams in those rare moments when I actually fall asleep... it's exhausting. I swear the clock on the bedside table is broken. Either that or time has slowed down. This could be the longest night of my adult life, and I had plenty of those in the Air Force.

If I'm honest with myself, I do know what's going on. No matter how hard I try to suppress my feelings, they come back stronger than ever. This has got to be causing an impressive spike in my stress level as well as blood pressure. Dr. Kim wouldn't be happy.

I'm a bottom line guy so out with it. I don't want to go back to Gulf Breeze. I want my truck. I want the freedom I once had to go and do what I please when I please. Is that too much to ask? Yes, I have dementia and the episodes occur more often as I get older. Surely there is a medication that I haven't tried yet that will make those damn fogs disappear for good. That's what I need to get back on track.

Russell has no idea that he triggered a relapse in me. I had convinced myself that I was fine with living at Gulf Breeze, going to meals with Blackjack, Maisey, and Frank. Flying my airplane. Starting each day with a crossword puzzle and coffee. Talking to him the other day made me realize that we're alike... we both moved here at about the same time, I've just made more strides in coping with the many changes. In time he might adjust like I think I have, or maybe not.

Anyway, I'm certain there is no returning to the safe and predictable life I've been living for the past seven months. Gulf Breeze is a fine place and the right choice for many of its elderly residents... but I have nagging doubts about me.

Come Sunday evening, I'm not going back. Sorry, Sarah, this will be hard on you. I promise to try harder to keep my wits about me and put a damper on the fogs. I believe if I really concentrate this time, I can make that happen. Please give me another chance.

I suppose I'm being selfish. My heart's in the right place, though, because I can better fulfill my roles as a father and grandfather without so many constraints. I'd trade anything to still be a husband, yet nothing will bring back Rebecca. I grieve every day. When I look at Justin, I see a resemblance to Rebecca, so I know she lives on in him.

God, I wish I could fall asleep. I'm so tired. What was that? The hint of a distant memory is teasing me. The next time it passes through my brain I'm going to grab onto it. Wait, wait, there it is. Got it.

Rebecca was in the hospital for an extended round of chemotherapy to treat her cancer. I was home after spending an exhausting night on the sofa-sleeper in her room. Sarah brought food over and watched me methodically put one bite of meatloaf after another into my mouth. Suddenly she perked up and said she had a job for me. Would I spend Saturday with Justin, who was five at the time?

I didn't think I was up to it. Sarah insisted, though, and made the good point that Justin missed his grandparents of late.

I took young Justin to the Galveston Mall, which was ironic since that was the scene of my much talked about misadventure years later. Anyway, we went to a toy store where I bought him a stuffed dinosaur before heading toward the food court, always a crowd favorite. On the way we walked by a display of kiddie rides. The mechanical type that gobbles quarters. Justin left my side and climbed aboard a helicopter, which was fitting since his grandpa was ex-Air Force.

While Justin bucked and swayed on the chopper, my mind drifted to my wife. She would have loved this outing with J-Man. I went to a dark place and sobbed quietly. I didn't even notice when Justin's ride ended and he was standing next to me, his hand on my arm.

I snapped out of my funk and asked him how he liked flying a helicopter. Was he having fun? He got a huge smile and said riding the helicopter and being with me was the best day of his life. I lost it and broke down. So many emotions in those days.

Fast forward fifteen years and Justin is fast asleep in the bedroom next to mine. He still likes being with me, which is a pleasant surprise because I've become an old man who'd never win an Oscar for portraying a happy camper.

Ok, enough mental rambling. Time to close my eyes for some much-needed sleep. Morning will be here in... a couple of hours. I have a big announcement to make at breakfast. Fortuitous that tomorrow... today... is Sunday.

There'll be a whole lot of praying going on very soon.

Chapter 22

Kenny awoke to the aroma of bacon. He got up, splashed water on his face, and stumbled into the kitchen where Sarah and Justin were sipping coffee and talking. He helped himself to a cup from the old percolator and raised his mug in greeting.

"Good morning, Dad, how did you sleep?" said Sarah.

"I tossed and turned a lot. Guess I wasn't used to that bed."

Justin said he heard Kenny through the wall, talking and moaning like he was in pain.

"I almost came in to check on you a couple of times, but always fell back asleep. I'm glad to see you're okay. I would've felt terrible if you needed help."

Kenny changed the subject by asking when breakfast would be ready. Sarah said it was ready now and for them to take a seat at the kitchen table. Sarah peppered her son with questions about his engineering studies and social life. Justin knew where she was headed and made a preemptive strike.

"Mom, I don't have much time to date. It seems like all I do is study and participate in Corps of Cadets activities," said Justin. "If I meet a coed engineering major who belongs to the Corps, and is rich and beautiful, you'll be the first to know. Don't hold your breath."

Kenny laughed and put his hand on Justin's shoulder.

"Take it from me, kid, don't stress out over finding Miss or Ms. Perfect. She's out there and she's looking for you, too. Your paths will cross one day and the wait will have been well worth it."

"Is that how it was with you and Grandma?" said Justin.

Kenny paused long enough for Sarah to chime in and warn her father that if he didn't answer Justin's question truthfully, she would.

"Well, it goes like this," said Kenny. "I was on a weekend pass with some buddies from Lackland Air Force Base. We were going from bar to bar in downtown San Antonio when I remembered my mother's birthday was days away. I told the guys I'd catch up with them and went into a JCPenney store.

"A very attractive and helpful clerk noticed I was a fish out of water in the women's department and offered her assistance. I bought a silk scarf that day from my future wife. It just happened."

Sarah admitted his story was accurate except for one omission: his Air Force friends tracked him down in JCPenney and the budding romance between Kenny and Rebecca almost ended right on the spot.

"Why is that?" said Justin. "It sounded like you two were getting along just fine."

"We'd all been drinking that afternoon and were on the prowl," said Kenny. "When my buddies found me, they were rather boisterous to put it mildly. They told me to hurry up so we could check out a strip club they'd heard about."

Sarah finished the story–she'd heard it many times from her mother.

"Grandma sold Grandpa the scarf and excused herself to help another customer. Your grandfather returned to JCPenney every chance he could for several weeks... by himself. Eventually Grandma agreed to go out with him, and the rest is history."

"Good story," said Justin. "These days I'm more likely to meet someone online than in a store. I shop a lot on Amazon so that about eliminates the store approach."

"Don't worry, honey, you have your whole life ahead of you. More eggs?"

Justin said his goodbyes and left for Texas A&M on Sunday afternoon. He had a research paper due and wanted to spend the evening tweaking its contents.

Kenny commented on what a fine young man Justin was and how his visit was special. Sarah agreed and told Kenny something he already knew, that the absence of Justin's father had taken its toll.

"Justin feels abandoned by his father," she said. "I'm doing the best I can to bridge the parenthood gap, but it's not the same. I am so thankful that you're a strong male role model for Justin. He needs you... I need you."

"I understand how difficult it must be to essentially raise a child on your own, hold down a job, and look after me. I admire how well you're doing all of that," said Kenny. "I also realize that my living with you only added to your challenges.

That makes what I have to say now the perfect storm of poor timing. I'm not going back to Gulf Breeze."

Sarah's mouth dropped open in disbelief. She stammered before finally getting the words out.

"What? Is this a joke? What on earth are you talking about, Dad?"

Kenny cleared his throat and forced himself to make eye contact with Sarah.

"No joke. "I'm better now. I know I can make it here this time. I won't be a burden."

Sarah raised her voice and pointed out that he was better *because* of his care at Gulf Breeze. The stability, treatment, medication, and oversight by staff all contributed to his improvement. For the first time in years, he had friends and a social life, she emphasized.

"I met a guy at Gulf Breeze. Name's Russell," said Kenny. "Listening to him talk about how he's lost control of his life, I realized that I feel the same way, always have. The only difference between us is I fooled myself and others into thinking I was happier. I'm not. I want to come home."

"Russell? I've never heard you mention his name," she said. "You need to stay away from him. He sounds like a bad influence. Have you talked with Frank or Blackjack? They know what you're thinking?"

Kenny told Sarah it was only right that she was the first to know his plan.

"Well, you're going to have to change your plan because you cannot move back. I work full-time and can't watch you day-to-day. Besides, I don't have the training to take care of you. Your memory lapses–fogs–are way beyond my ability to monitor and treat. C'mon, Dad."

Kenny clammed up. He sat on the couch and lowered his head. It wasn't too late to change his mind and tell Sarah it was a bad joke, he thought. No, he was serious.

Chapter 23

Sarah called her dental office at six o'clock Monday morning. No one would arrive until seven, which was fine with her. She wasn't in the mood for explaining in real time her situation with Kenny. A short message left on the office recorder would have to do.

"Okay, Dad, I just called work to say I'd be late. How late am I going to be? You ready to go back to Gulf Breeze?"

Kenny shook his head. He'd slept like a baby and felt clear-headed and alert.

"No, sweetie, I'm staying. You go to work and I'll putt around here until your shift is over. Go on now, I'll be just fine."

"Dammit, Dad, do you care about my situation at all? This isn't all about you. I have a huge emotional stake in your well-being, and moving home is absolutely the wrong thing for you to do."

Kenny went to the kitchen to get another cup of coffee, leaving Sarah exasperated and torn between crying and yelling. After leaving messages for Lucy and Dr. Kim to call her ASAP, she helped herself to a coffee refill, then turned and faced her father.

"Daddy, you can't be serious about staying here, can you? You need the special care of the memory unit at Gulf Breeze. You've had more lapses since moving there.

Remember falling asleep in the hallway and the trip to the mall? Please, be reasonable."

"I swear to God, Sarah, I will try harder than ever to control my fogs," said Kenny. "I know if I really concentrate on what I do each day, I can manage my behavior. I beg you, let me stay."

Sarah's mobile phone chirped. It was a text message from Dr. Kim, who was in Dallas for a two-day medical convention. She said she'd call on her next break unless it was an emergency. Sarah replied that it was urgent, but not an emergency. As soon as she hung up, Lucy called. She listened while Sarah explained what had transpired over the weekend.

"Wow, nobody saw that coming," said Lucy. "I know about Russell. He's a real complainer and regularly lodges complaints at the office. We need to talk your father off the ledge. I have an idea."

An hour later the Gulf Breeze shuttle parked on Sarah's driveway. Kenny had heard the large vehicle and was watching from the living room window as Lucy, Blackjack, Frank, and a male nurse walked to the front door. He opened the door before they could knock and rather brusquely asked what they were up to. Sarah pushed herself between Kenny and the visitors and invited them inside. The intervention quickly got under way.

Kenny made his case for wanting to leave Gulf Breeze. As an experienced administrator, Lucy listened politely, nodding her head as Kenny rambled on about losing his independence. Blackjack wasn't buying much, if any, of Kenny's diatribe.

"Lookee here, Puzzle Man, you got this all wrong," said Blackjack. "I remember when you were new at Gulf Breeze. You kept to yourself and hardly said a word. The only time I saw you was at a meal or when you were working a crossword puzzle. You call that living?"

Frank concurred with Blackjack. He said Kenny had done a radical turnaround since coming to Gulf Breeze.

"You're a different guy now," said Frank. "On your own you've met so many neighbors. Flying your drone airplane has made you a celebrity. People now know you as Kenny Boone, not so much as Puzzle Man. I call that progress."

Lucy cut to the chase by reminding Kenny that his dementia was becoming more serious and required constant monitoring and care. She said he couldn't expect his daughter to do that considering she was not specially trained and worked full-time.

"Daddy, we all want what's best for you," said Sarah, choking up as she talked. "Are you listening to what we're all saying? You're a smart man, you have to know that moving home is not an option."

Kenny stood and walked toward the bedroom he was using.

"Y'all have a nice ride back to Gulf Breeze," he said. "I'm taking a nap."

They all sat in silence as Kenny left the room. It was clear to Sarah that Kenny wasn't swayed by their strong argument for returning to Gulf Breeze.

"Wait, Kenny," Frank hollered. "I almost forgot. I brought you the daily crosswords from the weekend."

Kenny stopped in his tracks. The look on his face was noticed by all when he turned toward Frank. Sarah would recall later that her father's expression changed from defiant to determined. She didn't know at the time, but the crossword puzzles triggered a reaction that was both unexpected and welcomed. Kenny announced that he'd changed his mind and would return to Gulf Breeze... for the time being.

Kenny took the puzzles from Frank and went to his room to pack. He admitted to himself that seeing the puzzles had a stronger impact than Russell's influence. There was unfinished business to handle: identify and, if possible, assist the mystery puzzler. It was time to get back to work.

"Thanks for coming to the rescue," said Sarah. "Especially you, Frank. How did you know my dad would change his mind because of the puzzles?"

"Actually, I didn't know. It was a Hail Mary on my part. I'm just glad it worked."

Chapter 24

Three days back from his stay at Sarah's, another clue awaited Kenny in the morning's puzzle: *don't leave me.* Powerful stuff. Like he did with every clue he received, Kenny put the newspaper puzzle on his hall closet shelf after writing the clue on a master list. Eventually, he'd scrutinize all of them, searching for a pattern.

This morning he sat down in the game room to do the puzzle when a chair scraped on the floor beside him. Frank knew that Kenny didn't like to be disturbed but took a chance at getting reprimanded to talk with his friend.

"You seem to have settled back into a routine since last weekend," said Frank. "I gave you some space the past few days, but I can't wait any longer. Kenny, what's going on with you?"

Kenny looked around to ensure they had privacy and then spoke to Frank in a low voice.

"This doesn't go any further than the two of us, understand? I know I can trust you, Frank."

"Cross my heart, Kenny."

Kenny told him about the messages left in the newspaper puzzles and showed him the one from today. Someone was reaching out to Kenny for a reason he couldn't fathom. At first, Kenny said, he thought it was a bad joke. As time went on, though, he'd become convinced that a Gulf Breeze resident was in need of help. Why this person didn't just come out and ask was a big unknown.

Frank got coffee for them both and returned to the game room.

"No breakfast for me this morning," he said. "I've lost my appetite. Go on with your story."

Kenny took a sip and wiped his lips. "When I accepted the notion that the messages were legitimate cries for help, I decided to play detective and figure out the identity of who I call the mystery puzzler."

Frank interrupted to clarify if that was what was behind Kenny meeting his neighbors... suddenly becoming outgoing.

"Yes, that's been my motive all along. Of course, I didn't meet everyone at Gulf Breeze, but I did made a stab at putting together a short list of likely candidates. I then met with four married couples and a single man under the pretense of making new friends. Nobody suspects what I'm doing."

Frank asked where Kenny goes from here. "How will you learn who's leaving the messages unless you catch the person in the act?"

"Good question," said Kenny. "As of today, I don't have an answer. Keep an eye on them, get to know them better, wait for someone to slip up and leave a clue. Beats me. Any ideas?"

"Not at the moment. I'll think about it and let you know if I come up with anything," said Frank. "This is kind of exciting. Adds a little spice to an otherwise uneventful routine at Gulf Breeze. Consider me deputized."

Kenny laughed and told Frank he felt better about sharing his situation with a friend. The two vets had a lot in common with similar interests and perspectives.

"So what was going through your mind last weekend when you wanted to move back in with your daughter?"

Kenny got serious when he said he still wanted to return home.

"I've postponed my plans, that's all. I'm obsessed with finding the mystery puzzler because I have a strong feeling that time is running short for the puzzler and me. My biggest fear is having a fog and never coming out of it."

Frank put his arm around Kenny's shoulders and told him he'd always be there for him, as a wingman, deputy and friend.

Chapter 25

Kenny avoided Russell as best he could. He didn't want to risk falling under the man's spell again and disrupting his investigation into the mystery puzzler. Russell must have sensed the change in Kenny because now he was the one pursuing companionship.

"Kenny, there you are," said Russell. "I haven't seen you for a few days. I thought you'd busted out of this joint without saying goodbye."

"No, just had a weekend pass to stay with my daughter. How could I not come back to meatloaf and bingo nights?"

"I hope you're kidding. Hey, I got a hankering for catfish and fries. Let's skip lunch here today and go get some."

Kenny shook his head. "You know I'm on partial lockdown. I can't go with you unless a nurse's aide accompanies us. You up for that? I'm not."

Russell wasn't either.

"You stay here and eat an egg salad sandwich or whatever's on the menu," said Russell. "I'm going out. Be a good boy and obey the rules. Want me to bring you anything?"

Kenny declined the offer and went back to his room. The first set of neighbor notes he reread were from his initial meeting with Russell. The man was an enigma to Kenny; on the one hand, he was the poster child for living independently, while on the other hand, he still resided at Gulf Breeze.

Kenny had let Russell get under his skin and stir up nagging doubts about his own happiness. Kenny was well aware of his dementia and its impact on his life. He could talk a good game about living freely, like Russell, but the reality was he needed special medical care. Russell didn't have his restrictions, Kenny rationalized, although COPD was serious. As long as Russell had tanks of oxygen, he was fairly mobile. It simply was apples and oranges.

Moving on, Kenny shuffled through the remainder of his notes and reordered the ranking of possible mystery puzzlers. It was a toss-up between a half-dozen of the residents he'd visited. Where to go from here was something he could discuss with Frank.

Kenny stopped by the front desk and arranged for a nurse's aide to go with him and Frank to the vacant lot to fly the drone aircraft. Frank was manning the controls when Lucy appeared at Kenny's side.

"I heard you and Frank were out flying today," she said. "You doing okay?"

Kenny glanced at her while keeping an eye on his plane. "If you're referring to last weekend, yes, I'm doing okay. You've been talking about me with Sarah and Dr. Kim?"

Lucy said yes, several conversations in fact. The three caretakers talked at length about Kenny's surprise decision to move home. They'd all been impressed with his progress since coming to Gulf Breeze and wondered what caused him to regress.

"Something brought on your change of heart," said Lucy. "Is there anything I can do to restore your satisfaction with Gulf Breeze?"

"I have no problem with Gulf Breeze. You and the other staffers have been very sensitive to my needs and moods. No complaints from me. I guess after eight months I'm still adjusting. I may never be fully comfortable here. With dementia, my options are limited."

They stood in silence until Frank walked over and handed the controller to Kenny, who then turned to Lucy and asked if she wanted to fly the plane. Lucy declined and said perhaps another time. She had to get back to work.

"What was that all about, Kenny?" said Frank. "I only heard bits and pieces. Sounded serious."

"She was checking up on me. Nice lady. In about ten minutes she'll be on the phone to Dr. Kim and Sarah with a summary of our chat."

Frank wondered what she'd tell them.

"That I'm back, but not all the way."

Chapter 26

Kenny talked himself out of follow-up room visits with the four couples on his mystery puzzler short list. Instead he decided to casually "bump into them" at meals, on walks and other routine occasions. Spending time with Russell wasn't a problem. The rebel with a cause had found a reluctant kindred spirit in Kenny, and frequently sought him out.

He found Carol in the bistro nursing an iced tea. She invited him to sit with her and without asking ordered him a tea of his own. Carol explained that she didn't like to drink alone, even if it was a nonalcoholic beverage.

"This is my favorite part of the day... when Walter takes his afternoon nap. It's the only break I get from being his caretaker. I love him and all that, but geesh!"

"When Rebecca was in hospice it about drove me crazy because there was nothing I could do except hold her hand and talk to her," said Kenny. "You're lucky that Walter is physically and mentally agile for his age."

Carol looked at Kenny over the top of her glass. She asked if he and Rebecca were equal partners in their marriage or did one of them dominate. Kenny said it was fairly even in all matters other than his career and housing. When the Air Force said transfer, the family transferred.

"It's a seventy-thirty relationship in my marriage," said Carol. "I'm the seventy. Walter is a pretty upbeat man because I've always taken care of us. I suppose I haven't done him any favors by shielding him all these years, but he is emotionally fragile. He's gone to a psychologist for as long as we've been together."

Kenny was surprised to hear this about Walter and Carol. When he met with them in their unit, the couple enjoyed light-hearted bantering. She always got the last word, it seemed, and the back-and-forth often ended with a snappy command or retort by Carol.

"I would never have known that about you two," said Kenny. "On the surface you seem like happy, well-adjusted people."

"We've got our act down pat," she said. "The truth is I'm worn out from bolstering him all of these years. I thought by moving to Gulf Breeze I'd finally get the care and attention I need. Nothing's changed other than we live in a smaller place and somebody else prepares the meals."

Kenny finished his tea and asked if there was anything he could do to help her situation.

"You're a good listener, Kenny. I appreciate that very much. No, this is between me and Walter. It always has been. The only relief will be if I die before him. Oh my God, I can't believe I said that. Please disregard that last statement."

Kenny told her he would, but he knew he couldn't.

Chapter 27

"Say, Kenny, I saw you with a woman in the bistro yesterday," said Frank. "She married?"

"Yes, she's married and whatever your next question is, forget it. Carol is on my mystery puzzler list and I was only trying to get more information about her. She's definitely a contender."

Frank suggested that he tag along on future meetings, particularly those with women, to give Kenny another source of evaluating the puzzler finalists. Kenny told him changing the dynamics at this point could be awkward; he preferred to go it alone.

Frank shrugged and said Kenny couldn't blame him for trying.

"Go it alone then," said Frank. "Two-on-one meetings would probably raise red flags, anyway. I'll tell you what, you can use me as a sounding board going forward. You know, profile your mystery puzzler contenders and I'll give you a second opinion. Might be helpful, eh?"

Kenny agreed. "I'll take you up on your offer, my friend. In the meantime, let's go to the office and see if a nurse's aide is available tomorrow to babysit us while we fly the drone. I'm thinking right after breakfast. The weather forecast calls for an early afternoon thunderstorm."

During the short walk Kenny spotted Bert and Yvonne waiting for the shuttle by the main entrance. He introduced

Frank and then asked where they were going. Yvonne said she was going to pick up some medications while Bert stayed behind.

"I was late to our wedding and ever since she's been paying me back big time," said Bert. "Today it's the pharmacy, tomorrow it may be Las Vegas."

"Quit whining, Bert. You like it when I leave because you can cheat on your diet without me catching you. Now stay out of trouble and I'll see you in a couple of hours."

The three men stood in silence for a moment, until Kenny had what he considered to be a terrific idea: Bert could tag along with he and Frank while they flew the plane. Frank could be the pilot today, giving Kenny an opportunity to get up close and personal with Bert.

"Bert, you busy tomorrow morning?" said Kenny.

Frank was becoming quite the accomplished pilot, Kenny observed. He might have to change his friend's unofficial title from wingman to co-pilot.

"Atta boy, Frank. You're ready to buy a plane of your own. Imagine us putting on an aerial acrobatics demonstration for Gulf Breeze. We'd never have to pay for another prune juice as long as we live."

Bert wondered if he could try his hand at being a pilot. Kenny told him that it's a lot harder than it looked and required several lessons before Bert could man the controls on his own.

"So why did you invite me today if I don't get to fly?" said Bert. "I could have watched from a top floor window."

Frank overheard the conversation and reminded Bert that he's better off with them than sneaking snacks while his wife was shopping. Bert had diabetes.

Kenny said he and Frank were just being neighborly by including Bert in today's outing. As long as they were together, might as well get to know each other better. He asked Bert about his health and Yvonne's rheumatoid arthritis.

"No change for me since you met with us," said Bert. "Yvonne is another story. Her condition is worsening, and she refuses to admit it. She brushes it off as God's will. You may have picked up that I don't buy into all of that."

"What can you do?" said Kenny. "Yvonne sounded to me like she is totally fine with letting things take their natural course. You don't feel that way?"

Bert shook his head. He looked around to see if Frank was within earshot and then turned back to Kenny and whispered "no." Apparently, he never bought into God's will if it meant discounting medical treatment and rehabilitative programs. Yvonne used to be a fighter, he explained, but as her condition turned south, she turned to religion.

"Don't get me wrong, I'm a spiritual man. I'm also a realist who believes that God helps those who help themselves. Yvonne is in so much pain. I can't help her anymore. She won't let me."

Kenny bit his lip and thought over Bert's story. So, it was an act when they'd first met. Bert was an unwilling accomplice to his wife's chosen path forward. It had to be eating him up inside.

"By respecting Yvonne's wishes and supporting her philosophy on life... and death, I've lost much of my own zest for living," he said. "I think a lot about how much longer I can keep up this act when I see her slipping away. I just hope when the time comes, I'll be strong enough to do the right thing."

Kenny didn't ask for clarification of Bert's last comment. It was disturbing and none of his business. Yet he knew from this point on he could never see Bert and Yvonne together and not wonder what Bert meant by doing the right thing.

Frank announced that the two plane batteries were depleted, and they should head back to Gulf Breeze. The nurse's aide brought up the rear, Kenny and Frank walked together, and Bert led the way. Bert had nothing to say, prompting Frank to nudge Kenny and give him a questioning look. Kenny mouthed "later."

Kenny went straight to his room for a mid-afternoon nap. Frank had wanted Kenny to tell him what he and Bert discussed in such a quiet and private manner.

"Not today, Frank."

Chapter 28

Kenny planned to spend the day in front of the television watching marathon coverage of the Pan American Games. First, as always, he retrieved the daily newspaper and opened it to the crossword puzzle page. Another message awaited him: *I'm desperate.*

Things were getting more intense with the mystery puzzler. Cries for help now had taken on a sense of urgency. Kenny didn't know what to make of the latest message, only that its tone had changed.

He was mulling over the message at breakfast when he spotted Herb and Barbara across the room. The couple had finished eating and walked by Kenny on their way out. He smiled and nodded; Herb was indifferent while Barbara squinted and pursed her lips as if to say something. She kept silent and followed her husband to the lobby area.

Ten minutes later Kenny pushed in his chair and started back to his room with the newspaper tucked under his arm. He caught a motion in the lobby and saw Barbara waving at him. Herb wasn't with her.

"Good morning, Barbara. Where's Herb?"

"He went to use a computer in the library. Probably to look up buying marijuana from Canada. He says if he has to live like this, he might as well be high."

Kenny asked her what Herb meant by "live like this."

She explained how since moving to Gulf Breeze several years ago, Herb had way too much time on his hands, time he used to feel sorry for himself. He was selfish in being so focused on his own misery and not hers, she said.

"Herb should be in Hollywood–he's a good actor. His career was underwhelming by any standards. Herb's brother was wildly successful in the stock market and is a constant reminder of Herb's thirty-five mediocre years in the insurance business. He is bitter, embarrassed, and refuses to accept responsibility for his own shortcomings."

Barbara went on to explain that on top of his career woes, Herb was the reason they could not have children. He spent years in denial and blaming her even though a battery of tests proved his sperm count was too low. Whenever she suggested adoption, he'd go ballistic.

"He wanted nothing to do with adopting," said Barbara. "Herb was hung up on having a biological child of his own. And get this, it was my fault."

Kenny saw the tears welling up in Barbara's eyes and decided this conversation had gotten way too heavy. He apologized and was about to leave when she whirled and faced him, shaking with emotion.

"Listen to me. I have no one to talk to about my miserable life. You seem like an honorable man, a trustworthy man... a veteran. I want someone to know what I'm dealing with here. Some days I think I'd do anything to change my life."

Kenny was floored and momentarily speechless. At last he managed to tell Barbara to be strong and persevere, two characteristics he acquired in the service and in trying to adapt to Gulf Breeze. She wondered if that is what he'd do if their positions were swapped.

"I don't know what I'd do, to be honest. I'm not sure I want to know."

Chapter 29

Dr. Kim finished examining Kenny and had him take a seat in the waiting area while she talked to Sarah. He flipped through a six-month-old copy of *Elle* and tossed it aside when another patient smiled and winked at his choice of reading material.

"You ready to go, Dad?" said Sarah.

"More than ready. Can we grab lunch before you take me back to my cell? I don't feel like split pea soup and Jell-O salad today."

Sarah took him to a hole in the wall that specialized in shrimp and grits. Kenny washed it down with a Shiner beer. He remarked that the meal would keep him in fine fiddle until dinner. Before they left the restaurant, Kenny wanted to know what Dr. Kim had to say about him.

"We're both concerned about your fogs," she said. "They are occurring more often and lasting longer than this time a year ago. It's to be expected, Dr. Kim pointed out, as a natural progression of dementia. We are happy that you seem happier at Gulf Breeze after your meltdown at home a while back."

Kenny finished his iced tea and stared out at the traffic along the sea wall that separated Galveston from the beach.

"Everybody's happy, that's good news," said Kenny. "I'm keeping busy with my puzzles and airplane. My friend Frank is almost as adept at flying as me. Things are at a steady state with me, except for the damned fogs. Does Dr. Kim think I'll ever have one and never come out of it?"

Sarah studied her father. "She's never mentioned that scenario, but I suppose it could happen. Does that bother you?"

"Hell, yes, it bothers me," said Kenny. "I could end up in la la land and not even know it. I suppose that could be a blessing in some situations. I try really hard to stay in the moment. Then I have another fog. I'm not ready for the drool cup."

Sarah laughed and said she hoped he never lost his dry sense of humor. She thought to herself how his humor might be the key to him keeping a grip on his declining health until... he couldn't.

The conversation during the ride to Gulf Breeze was mostly about Sarah's job and Justin's progress at Texas A&M. Kenny was tired of talk about himself—it went against the grain of his humble manner to be in the spotlight.

"Here we are, Dad. Home safe and sound. I'm going to wait in the car while you walk in just to make sure you don't make a run for it. Kenny pecked Sarah's cheek and walked through the double glass door. As Sarah drove off he pushed the door to exit and halted when Lucy's chipper voice called out to welcome him back to Gulf Breeze.

"Busted again by Parole Officer Lucy," he sighed. "Just my luck you were in the lobby."

"No luck at all," she said. "Your daughter texted me from the restaurant. I've been expecting you, Mr. Boone."

Chapter 30

The fourth chance encounter Kenny arranged was with Stan and Margaret–both of them rather than only a husband or wife like the other three couples. It shouldn't be too difficult, he reasoned, since they were diehard *Jeopardy* watchers who could be found watching the facility's big-screen television every weekday afternoon.

Kenny strolled into the TV room just as residents were settling in for an episode. He spotted the couple and sat directly behind them. He tapped them on the shoulders and said hello. They were curt in their responses, which Kenny assumed was because the show had begun. He'd wait for the first commercial break.

A pillow ad was in full swing as Kenny leaned forward and began the small talk. He knew right away that having a productive conversation in two minute spurts wasn't happening. During the break before the double jeopardy round, he invited Stan and Margaret for a drink in the tiny Gulf Breeze bar.

"'This is a bit of a surprise for us," said Stan. "First, you appear at our door, then you sit behind us during a game show, and now you invite us to join you for cocktails. You're not a stalker, are you?"

Margaret scolded her husband for being rude. She said other residents could learn from Kenny's friendliness.

Kenny hoped that the dim lighting hid his blushing face. Again, he felt sneaky about his motive for pursuing the identity of the mystery puzzler. It was for a good cause, he reasoned–helping someone in need justified the deception.

"Actually, I was looking for my friend, Frank, and thought he might be here with the other devoted Alex Trebek fans," said Kenny. "I didn't see him, but I did see you two. I thought it'd be fun to catch up on things."

"See, Stan, Kenny is a nice man. Don't be so suspicious," said Margaret.

They found an empty table in the bar and chatted about their health, quality of food at Gulf Breeze, families, and news of the day. A mass casualty shooting in Idaho earlier in the week continued to be the top story in the media. A disgruntled worker who was fired for stealing from his employer went home, got an assault rifle, and returned to the factory where he worked to get revenge, the authorities stated. He then took his own life.

"The guy was a wacko who did us all a favor by killing himself," Stan said. "Think about it, someone could go nuts at Gulf Breeze and do the same thing. You know, a resident who'd had it with *Jeopardy* and instead wanted to watch *Family Feud* in the media room. But he got outvoted and was pissed."

Margaret and Kenny stared at Stan for a moment before Margaret reacted.

"Yeah, it could happen. I just hope if it does, the psycho either misses me or makes a kill shot. Quick and painless, I say. Is that too much to ask?"

Stan nodded in agreement. "You're right, Margaret. Life boils down to one day at a time and, excuse my French, shit happens. What're you gonna do?"

Kenny took note of the couple's honest view of the world, even if it was, well, somewhat doomsday. They dealt with whatever came their way without pretenses. He decided that neither were strong candidates as mystery puzzler. They did make for interesting drinking partners, however.

"One more round, on me," said Kenny.

Diary: August 14

Wow, that was enlightening. I accomplished what I set out to do in the second round of mystery puzzler evaluations. I've narrowed the list of probables to Carol, Bert, Yvonne, and Barbara. Russell is on some other kind of list only because I find him amusing and intriguing. He's like being around me when I was new at Gulf Breeze. I find myself watching and listening to him as he rants about the restrictions here and about wanting to bust out. Was that me at one time? Is it still me deep inside?

Lucy told me that I had a mild fog not too long ago in the dining room. I didn't eat anything, just sat there and stared into space like a zombie. Must have scared the heck out of Maisey. I'm almost sorry I didn't pick up on Blackjack's comments as they would have been hilarious.

Frank told me later that he called for a nurse to escort me to my room where I spent the next ten hours in the recliner. I woke up with no memory of the episode and really hungry. Sarah and Dr. Kim visited me, but I have no idea what we talked about.

It's a good thing I keep notes about the mystery puzzler candidates because if I had to rely on memory there'd be very little to recall. Somehow Russell heard of my dining room sideshow and came around to check me out. I know he can be a negative influence, but I enjoy our one-sided conversations in which he recruits me to break house rules. For a short time, I get to pretend I'm the rebel I once was through Russell.

What's next? I haven't come up with a plan for moving my puzzler investigation forward. I've got names and motives, which to a good cop would be enough to hone my list further. But I'm a retired Air Force mechanic with no training in criminology or social science.

Best I can do under the circumstances is continuing to watch the final four without being obvious. "Chance" meetings, discreet eavesdropping on their conversations, observe their body language, and anything else I can come up with in my role as amateur sleuth.

Frank wonders if he can be more than a sounding board. I will give that serious thought. He is able and willing while I'm... unpredictable.

The puzzle messages are sporadic but appearing more often. I still cannot decipher if they are requests for assistance or more serious life-and-death pleadings. I have to assume the latter. Underestimating the messages could have fatal consequences.

Focus, Kenny. Fight through the fogs. And for God's sake, man, hurry up.

Chapter 31

Blackjack had what he called a "great idea." He suggested at dinner that Kenny join him, Maisey, and Frank on a shuttle trip to nearby Moody Gardens. The world famous complex was founded in 1986 to educate visitors about conservation and wildlife.

"We want to see the Aquarium Pyramid–it has sharks, stingrays and other marine animals," said Blackjack. "I hear it's pretty awesome. What do you say, Puzzle Man, you in?"

Kenny paused. "I'll have to check with Lucy. If she can assign a nurse's aide to tag along, I'd like to go."

Blackjack hooted. "We'll call it the redemption field trip, to make up for your less than sterling experience at the Galveston Mall. You do remember that one, don't you?"

Frank told Blackjack to back off because it wasn't funny. Blackjack apologized to Kenny and muttered that it was kind of funny. Frank said he'd go on the trip if Kenny was able to secure a nurse's aide.

Lucy pulled some strings and Kenny got clearance and a medical escort for the half-day excursion to Moody Gardens. The aide was a sturdily built young man named Nick whose presence deterred Blackjack from his typical litany of wise-cracks.

It was a hot and humid day in Galveston. The shuttle van driver announced over the PA system that everyone needed to move slowly, seek shade when outdoors, and drink plenty of water. He'd return to Moody Gardens in four hours and for them to be on time for the return ride to Gulf Breeze.

Twenty-two residents exited the van and followed the signs to the destinations of their choosing. Kenny, Blackjack, Maisey, Frank, and about ten others walked toward the Aquarium Pyramid with Nick bringing up the rear. He carried a small backpack with water, sunscreen, and a mobile phone. The shuttle driver and Lucy were on speed dial.

They were settling into their seats for a 3D multi-media extravaganza about sharks and whales when Kenny felt a firm hand on his shoulder. He craned his neck and was surprised to see it was Russell.

"Russell, you missed the shuttle ride?"

"Yes, but I missed it on purpose," said Russell. "No way I was going to take the cattle car to Moody Gardens when I have my own wheels. You could have ridden with me, you know."

Kenny explained yet again that he had restrictions on traveling outside of Gulf Breeze. Hitching a ride in Russell's pickup truck didn't meet the criteria.

The movie began and conversation among the residents ceased except for the occasional oohs and aahs. Maisey recoiled when a great white shark appeared to swim straight at the audience with its teeth flashing. Russell let out a loud "look out!" that did as much to upset the people seated near him as the shark itself. Kenny couldn't help smiling–the guy was a pistol.

On their way out of the theater Russell matched pace with Kenny and Frank. He tempted Kenny with the offer to stop at a Whataburger drive-in on the return drive to Gulf Breeze. He said no and suggested that Frank join Russell and bring Kenny back some food. Russell had a change of heart and suggested some other time, he had errands to run.

Later, back at Gulf Breeze, Frank wanted Kenny's take on Russell. Kenny wondered why and Frank told him he found the man quite unusual, not at all fitting the mold of the other residents.

"I can't figure out the guy," said Frank. "He has disdain for all of us lifers, yet he lives here, too. If he dislikes it so much, why doesn't he leave? I would."

Kenny said there was more than meets the eye with Russell. He lowered his voice and told Frank that Russell was terminally ill.

"He's dying a slow death from COPD. When you don't see him around, he's in his room on oxygen. Russell is a proud man and doesn't want any pity. He does a good job of masking his illness and emotions."

"Man, you just never know about people, do you? I've heard him wheeze when he breathes but thought it might be allergies. I find it really sad that he's basically alone. It's nice that he latched on to you, Kenny, and that you've become his friend."

Kenny leveled his gaze at Frank. "Would it surprise you to learn that he is on my mystery puzzler list? At the bottom, five of five with a big question mark. It's a way for me to keep an eye on him. He seems too tough to harm himself, but as his health declines, you never know."

We'll watch him together," said Frank. "He could use another friend, for sure. Hell, we all could."

Chapter 32

Kenny felt like he'd made headway with the puzzler investigation. At the same time, he was increasingly frustrated by where to go from here. He considered getting up early and sitting in a dark corner of the game room in hopes of catching the person who was leaving the messages. Frank pointed out that it would be hit or miss and could take weeks. Neither had any other ideas.

There was another message today: *tick tock.* The meaning was clear, time was running out. He tucked the newspaper under his arm and went to eat breakfast. Oatmeal again. The transition from live-to-eat to eat-to-live had a firm hold on Kenny. He still enjoyed a good meal, but less so as he aged. The taste buds weren't what they used to be.

Blackjack and Maisey joined Kenny as he was finishing his meal. She had trouble getting words out due to her stroke, yet always gave Kenny a smile. He appreciated the effort.

"What's on your agenda today, Puzzle Man," said Blackjack. "When are you going to teach me how to fly your plane? I could be a distant relative of the Tuskegee Airmen, you ever think of that?"

Tuskegee Airmen was a group of African-American pilots who fought in World War II as part of the U.S. Army Air Forces. Blackjack might indeed be related to an airman; more likely he was name dropping to make an impression, Kenny thought.

"If you're serious, Blackjack, and follow my instructions, I'll show you how to fly the plane," said Kenny. He looked at Maisey and asked if she'd like to see her husband operating a plane. She raised her eyebrows.

"Okay, next time Frank and I go across the street to the vacant lot, we'll take you with us," said Kenny. "It'll be a challenge for me, but I believe I can make a Gulf Breeze Airman out of you, Blackjack. As long as you follow my orders."

Blackjack bristled and his mouth opened to speak. Uncharacteristically, he said nothing. Kenny smiled to himself at rendering the man speechless.

The knock on the door woke Kenny from a nap in his recliner. As he stood to answer the door, the mystery puzzler notes fell from his lap to the floor. He hurriedly picked them up and put the short stack upside down on the coffee table.

"Russell, what brings you here?" said Kenny. "Everything all right?"

Russell pushed past Kenny and walked to the sliding glass door. He had a pained look on his face. Kenny asked him to sit down and talk. Russell just stood glancing out to the street below, his head turning side to side.

"I came by to tell you I'm leaving. I want one person at Gulf Breeze to know I wasn't kidnapped or fell into a sewer opening. That person is you. I want you to promise me that when I go, you won't say anything for twenty-four hours. That will give me time to make a clean getaway."

Kenny stared at Russell. "You sound like you're a prisoner at Alcatraz. Remember the Clint Eastwood movie? You can leave anytime you want, why the dramatics?"

Russell helped himself to a beer from Kenny's fridge without offering the host one. He took a long drink, belched and held up his hand.

"You know I have COPD and my days are numbered," said Russell. "Sure, I could leave anytime except for one thing: my son got power of attorney while I was hospitalized earlier this year and he controls the purse strings. If I leave, I'll have no access to my own money, and I have a fair amount of it. I will be provided for as long as I'm institutionalized. It's blackmail if you ask me."

Kenny couldn't believe what he just heard. Sarah would never treat him that way. She wanted what was best for him while Russell's son was all about controlling his father and the purse strings. Russell said his choices were to either receive assisted living care at Gulf Breeze and continue to be unhappy until he died or leave and regain his freedom until he died... sooner.

"Why did your son let you keep your truck?"

"He has it all figured out," said Russell, getting another beer and this time bringing Kenny a Lone Star as well. "The truck is a concession to my personal freedom. He figures all I'll do is drive around Galveston because I can never be too far from my oxygen supply. So far he's right. But I have a surprise for him."

Russell went on to tell Kenny how he'd been saving money from the monthly draw his son established and had enough to pay for gas, food and lodging to get him to Flagstaff, Arizona. He'd read about a facility that did experimental treatment on patients with respiratory diseases in exchange for free medical care.

"What about your oxygen equipment? Could you last the two-to-three days it takes to drive to Flagstaff without the tanks and mask?"

Russell finished his beer and turned to leave. "I've already taken care of that. If you hear rumors of missing equipment, they're true. I have it under a tarp in my truck bed. Don't rat me out, Kenny."

"I'll honor the twenty-four hours you requested," said Kenny. "After that, I make no promises. I won't lie if I'm asked by authorities. When are you leaving? Soon?"

"I'm not going to tell you when I leave. You'll wake up one morning and I'll be gone. That's the way it has to be. The next time you see me will be in an open casket at my funeral if my son is willing to pay for it."

They shook hands and parted ways. Kenny went back to his recliner and shuffled through his notes. He found the section with Russell's information and put an asterisk next to the question mark at the top of the page. Then he closed his eyes.

Chapter 33

Kenny modified his morning ritual to include looking for Russell at breakfast along with working the crossword puzzle. He recruited Frank to be on the lookout for Russell without telling him the reason why. The next four mornings were like any other; the fifth was different. No Russell.

Frank met up with Kenny at lunch in the dining room. He said he hadn't seen Russell as yet and wondered if Kenny had.

"No, I haven't," said Kenny. "It's not like Russell to miss a meal. Maybe he decided to eat in town today. He does like Whataburger and Denny's."

"Yeah, that's probably it. Unless he's not feeling well and is resting in his room. Should we go and see?"

Kenny shook his head. "No, let's give him some privacy. He'll come down when he feels up to it. He always has before."

"You going to tell me why we're monitoring Russell?" said Frank.

"I may be able to tell you at breakfast tomorrow. That's the best I can do."

"What are you and Russell up to, Kenny?"

Russell had bypassed an exterior door alarm sometime in the middle of the night and drove away from Gulf Breeze undetected. Strapped securely in the truck bed were two cylinders of oxygen, a mask and tubing. Flagstaff was a 1,250-mile drive that'd take him north to Ft. Worth, west through Wichita Falls and Amarillo, and then continue on I-40 to Albuquerque, Winslow and Flagstaff. He'd planned to sleep in his truck at rest stops, obey the speed limit, and eat when and whatever he wanted. Russell told himself he might as well die at an elevation of 7,000 feet than at sea level.

Kenny was nervous at breakfast. Frank read his friend's discomfort and said he wanted to talk after the meal. They walked to the lobby together and took a seat on the overstuffed couch. Kenny waited until a few residents passed by then turned to Frank.

"I want you to accompany me to Russell's room. If he doesn't answer the door, go find Lucy or some other administrator and have them use their pass key to get into Russell's room. Will you do that?"

"Kenny, you promised to tell me what's going on," said Frank. "Out with it."

"I will tell you as soon as we find out if Russell is in his room."

"You suspect he might have died? That's why we haven't seen him lately?

"We'll know soon enough. Let's go to his room."

When three minutes of knocking and calling out to Russell didn't produce him, instead causing next door neighbors to ask about the racket, Kenny sent Frank to the office. Keep it quiet, Kenny said, no need to cause a panic.

Lucy and a nurse arrived with Frank in less than five minutes. Lucy knocked and then let herself in. The others followed behind. No Russell, but there was a note taped to the refrigerator: *I'm gone for good. Kenny can give you the details of my departure. Somebody let my son know about me, not that he'd care much. My action is no reflection on Gulf Breeze, this is a caring place; however, not the place I want to spend what time I have left. So long, adios, ciao and all that. Lord almighty, I'm free at last!*

All eyes turned to Kenny. He was choked up. Lucy gave him a moment and then insisted he tell them about Russell and how long he knew about Russell's plan to leave. Kenny related it all to Lucy, Frank and the nurse. He debated whether to tell them Russell was on his way to Flagstaff, but in the end, he felt it was the right thing to do.

Lucy said she'd contact the facility in Flagstaff after doing an online search. First, she needed to contact Russell's son, who no doubt would be quite upset that Gulf Breeze let his father run away. As if they could stop him.

"I'm going to talk to the state police in Texas, New Mexico and Arizona and see if they can locate him. We're assuming he'll arrive safely sometime today, yet anything could happen to him along the way."

Before they left the room, Lucy told Kenny he needed to come to the office and complete a formal report about Russell, and talk to Karen, the executive director of Gulf Breeze. Kenny wasn't in trouble, but there were questions that needed answering, she said.

Frank followed Kenny to his room, which was down the hallway from Russell's.

"You knew what Russell was going to do and you didn't tell anyone? What were you thinking, Kenny?"

"I know exactly how Russell was feeling. I left here not too long ago myself. Fortunately, I was running toward my daughter, while Russell was running away from his son. I had a home to go to–Russell has nothing like that. This is personal for me.

"I waited twenty-four hours before blowing the whistle. That's what he asked me to do. I don't apologize nor regret my small role in his departure."

Frank touched Kenny's arm and said he would have done the same thing and that he admired Kenny for his loyalty to Russell.

"Do you think we'll ever here from Russell?" said Frank.

"Honestly, I don't know. But I wouldn't be surprised if one day a postcard arrives from Flagstaff, Arizona. On the back will be a message along the lines of *Wish you were here! Miss me yet?* Guess what? I already miss him."

Chapter 34

It took Lucy two days to locate the place in Flagstaff where Russell went for free medical treatment. He'd arrived the day before, just in the nick of time, as his oxygen supply was dangerously low. She learned that Many Pines Treatment Center was not AMA approved and received no government funding. It limped along on private donations, and patients who could afford to pay their own way. Others, like Russell, were accepted on a space available basis as long as they agreed to experimental treatment.

Kenny was interrogated thoroughly by Gulf Breeze's Karen and Lucy. He sensed that was mostly about preparing for possible legal action by Russell's son, whom they'd clashed with in the past. Kenny felt like a scapegoat, but was okay with it. The only crime committed was the stolen oxygen equipment. He doubted the facility would press charges against Russell. That could be a PR nightmare if the story leaked to the media. Better to let it go.

Lucy said that in her discussion with Many Pines, she was told that contact between patients and the outside world was discouraged. The patients were there because they were desperate to get medical help, and many had lost confidence in support from family and mainline medical resources.

"Russell viewed Gulf Breeze as his last resort," said Kenny. "'The only place to go from here was a cemetery,' he used to say. Many Pines' treatment may extend his life. If not, it will at least allow him to go out on his own terms. That's important to him."

The meeting ended with everyone in the room depressed. The director asked Kenny if he'd agree to the company's position that Russell left to get specialized care in Arizona. No other details. And would he talk to Frank about doing the same?

"Yes, I'll do both," said Kenny. "It's the truth and you're not asking me to do any more than tell the truth. I think the less said the better."

Kenny found Frank and talked to him about the meeting. Frank was on board with the administrator's request for low-key handling of Russell's departure. Both men were somber and wanted some alone time. Frank suggested they meet in his room later for a few beers and to watch the Astros play the White Sox on TV.

Kenny took the long way to his room, passing by Russell's vacant unit. Empty boxes were neatly stacked in the hall in preparation for packing his belongings. In a matter of days there'd be a new tenant in room 223. *Life goes on,* he muttered.

Diary: September 16

I'm beat. The ordeal with Russell is a tough one for me. Deep inside I'm rooting for the guy...living the adventure through him with no risk on my part. Yes, it's selfish of me, I won't deny it.

Russell took a part of me with him to Flagstaff. We're kindred spirits, only he wanted his freedom more than me. My loving daughter and grandson have made it easier for me to adapt to life in an assisted care facility than Russell. He had nothing to go home to–no home at all, in fact–and no one waiting on the outside who gave a damn.

I try not to dwell on Russell and the experimental treatments he's undergoing. Unfortunately, I can't unsee the science fiction B movies where patients got injections of unknown serum that turned them into monsters. Even if the treatments don't do anything to ease his COPD, I pray to God they at least make life more comfortable.

Russell has been gone for five weeks. A nice married couple now resides in room 223. I don't have any interest in meeting them, at least not until more time passes.

As for my investigation into the identity of the mystery puzzler, it may be over. There has been no message in the daily newspaper since before Russell drove off. For a lot of reasons that are now clear, he must have been the one.

Russell reached out to me and I didn't make the connection. Some savior I turned out to be.

Chapter 35

The fog resembled the one that triggered a Silver Alert when Kenny parked his truck and walked along the Galveston seawall so many months ago. This time, his long walk was confined to the hallways of Gulf Breeze and instead of culminating on a public bench overlooking the ocean, he ended up in the library staring at a blank screen.

Lucy said residents recalled seeing him shuffling back and forth on the second floor–his floor and once Russell's. It was Frank who went looking for Kenny and found him seated in front of a computer monitor. Kenny was punching keys over and over, yet nothing appeared on the screen because it was turned off. Frank watched Kenny for a minute and then led him back to his room. He called Lucy who arrived shortly with a nurse in tow.

"I reached Dr. Kim and she'll be over as soon as she finishes with her appointments," said Lucy. "Sarah will time her visit with Dr. Kim's."

The nurse finished her examination of Kenny and reported that he was fine–considering. Per his other episodes, she said Kenny would likely sleep most of the day and wake up with little or no recollection of what had transpired.

Frank volunteered to stay with Kenny until Sarah and Dr. Kim arrived. He watched Fox News while Kenny dozed in his recliner. Every time Kenny talked in his sleep, obviously dreaming, Frank listened for words that might indicate what the dreams were about. He expected to hear Kenny mention Russell or puzzle, but all he could distinguish were "freedom" and "truck".

"By now, you must be in total agreement that Gulf Breeze is the right place for you, Dad, and that coming home with me is out of the question," said Sarah. She'd arrived a few minutes after Dr. Kim, who was listening to the interchange between father and daughter.

Kenny was still groggy, so it took him longer than usual to get up to speed in a conversation. He wanted to know how long he'd been in the fog. He didn't react to the response of eight hours.

"I'm in agreement, but not one hundred percent," he managed to get out. "There will always be part of me that regrets and resents the circumstances that put me here. Call it the 'Russell Factor.' This isn't home, it's where I live. Not to worry, I'm not going anywhere."

Dr. Kim said she was very happy to hear him say that, because he was in no condition to drive to Flagstaff like his friend, or even to the corner market. She saw the look on his face and quickly reminded him that he could continue to go on outings if he had a family or nurse escort. It was for his own safety as well as others, she said.

"Yeah, I get it. In the meantime, Dr. Kim, is there any adjustment you can make to my meds? I don't want to become a zombie, though, just something to help ward off the damn fogs."

Dr. Kim shook her head and said there was little wiggle room in his medications. If he was in pain, she could up the dosage, but that wasn't the case.

"Your dementia has a mind of its own, excuse the idiom. Your lapses or fogs occur randomly as a result of your illness and aging. The goals you're working on to eat right, exercise, socialize, and reduce stress are still the best way to go."

Sarah pointed out that her father had fallen way short on reducing stress lately, which could account for his latest fogs.

"This Russell thing really got to you, Dad," she said. "You've got to move on, seriously."

Dr. Kim concurred and suggested that Kenny be given a home visit soon. Maybe take in an Astros game–in person. She looked questionably at Sarah, who nodded.

"I'll see if Justin can come home from college and we'll have a family weekend."

Kenny thought it was a great idea. He said he needed to distance himself from the turmoil of Russell leaving Gulf Breeze and the guilt he felt for keeping Russell's Flagstaff plans a secret.

"A break in my routine will be just what the doctor ordered," he said, winking at Dr. Kim.

Chapter 36

The first thing Kenny did after a restful and enjoyable weekend with Sarah and Justin was to find Lucy and ask if she had an update on Russell. She did.

"He's alive, that's all I can tell you. Many Pines, like most experimental medical facilities, prefers to stay off the grid when it comes to publicity and communicating with outsiders. Patient privacy is one of the top reasons why terminal patients enroll in such a place."

Kenny wondered if Russell's son had been in contact with Many Pines to check on his father. Lucy did not know. She also said that efforts by Kenny to reach Russell likely wouldn't be successful. The Many Pines official with whom she spoke was very clear about that.

"I'm going to keep writing Russell," said Kenny. "It sounds like my letters may not reach him, but you never know. I want him to remember he has friends who are thinking of him."

Kenny paused, took a deep breath and continued. "It's ironic how he considered himself a 'prisoner' here and escaped only to end up in another prison. A high-elevation prison with more rules than Gulf Breeze. I pray he finds relief."

There had been no mystery puzzler messages since Russell's departure, which convinced Kenny that he was the one. Kenny was relieved to resume his morning routine without being confronted by another cry for help. Just him, the daily newspaper, and coffee.

Kenny yelped when he opened today's newspaper. There, in the familiar handwriting and horizontal-vertical placement of letters was *why me?* He grabbed the paper and went into the dining room to wait for Frank. His scrambled eggs got cold as he drank cup after cup of coffee and scanned the room for his friend. At last, Frank sauntered in and sat down.

"Frank, look at this," said Kenny. His hand holding the newspaper was shaking from nerves and caffeine.

"Another message. You were sure it was Russell because it'd been so long since the last one. Guess the puzzler is still among us at Gulf Breeze."

"It would appear so," said Kenny. "With Russell out of the picture, that leaves Carol, Bert, Yvonne, and Barbara as frontrunners. The investigation is back on."

Frank and Kenny were discussing next steps when Blackjack and Maisey joined them. Blackjack asked what the two men were talking about. From a distance, he said it appeared the topic was serious.

"We're having a friendly argument about the Houston Texans football team," said Frank. "Kenny says the defense needs beefing up and I say a top-level running back is more important. I think we're both right."

Kenny excused himself and went to the game room where he pored over the day's puzzle. Frank waited a few minutes and then joined him. They looked at each other before Frank asked what Kenny's next move was going to be.

"Resume our surveillance and analysis of the remaining four suspects," said Kenny.

Frank chuckled and remarked how Kenny sounded like a cop in a TV series.

"You're right," said Kenny. "'Suspects' is too harsh, more like 'persons of interest.'"

"You used the word 'our'. Does that mean you want me more involved in the investigation?"

"I do, because I don't know where to go from here," said Kenny. "I was so certain the mystery puzzler was Russell that I considered this matter to be over. I need your help so if you have any ideas, I'm open to them."

Frank thought about it for a minute before suggesting they stake out the game room early each morning until they witnessed the person leaving the messages. Black ops, he called it, sitting in a dark corner of the room behind the large globe and potted fern. One early morning duty, the next one off, then back again for as long as it took.

"That could take a while since there's no pattern of when the mystery puzzler strikes," said Kenny. "I like your idea and am grateful I don't have to pull early morning duty by myself. Let's start tomorrow, I'll go first."

Before he turned in for the night, Kenny made the necessary adjustments to the game room to ensure he'd be sufficiently concealed. Satisfied, he asked a roving security guard if he knew when the morning newspaper was delivered. The young man said usually between five and five-thirty weather permitting.

Kenny set his alarm clock for four-thirty but knew from experience he'd be awake well before then. The small coffee maker that Sarah bought for him had a built-in timer that he also set for four-thirty.

It wouldn't do for me to fall asleep and miss the mystery puzzler, he told himself. Go-cups of hot java were mandatory for this mission. He'd strongly recommend to Frank that he arrive at the game room with a steaming mug in hand.

Chapter 37

Kenny's first morning of surveillance was uneventful. The newspaper was delivered to the game room at five-twenty where it remained untouched until he retrieved it a little past six, which was the usual time he started working the daily puzzle. No one had entered the game room other than a housekeeper who dropped off the newspaper and left.

Kenny took the paper into the dining room to get another cup of coffee and was surprised to see Frank seated at table 14.

"I don't recall ever seeing you here this early," said Kenny. "You especially hungry this morning?"

"Hungry for a fruit cup and slice of toast? Nope. I'm anxious to find out what happened this morning in the game room. Any luck?"

Kenny showed him the blank puzzle and shook his head. "Not today. Maybe you'll have better luck tomorrow."

"Something tells me we'll be spending a lot of mornings in the game room," said Frank. "We need to come up with a 'plan B.'"

Kenny was onboard with a backup plan whatever it might be. He realized that waiting for the mystery person to reveal him or herself was simply wishful thinking. He and Frank had to force the issue to make it happen.

"Let's keep doing the surveillance until we catch the puzzler, or we are tired of getting up early," said Kenny. "At least sitting alone in a dark corner of the game room gives us an opportunity to brainstorm ideas. Thank God for coffee."

Frank was good with that suggestion. It wasn't exactly a "plan B"; more like a plan to come up with a real "plan B." He told Kenny he wanted to read the seven messages to date, so they went to his room where Kenny retrieved the master list from the closet. He'd labeled each message by name and date, referring to them as clues.

"I can tell that those cop and lawyer shows you like so much are paying off," said Frank. "Did you complete the puzzles that have messages? I see you have them stacked on the shelf."

Kenny said he did not work on those puzzles, preferring to leave them pristine.

"Notice how I keep them in baggies? That's to preserve fingerprints and DNA from the mystery puzzler. Call me paranoid, but I have learned a lot watching the CSI series."

"You need to get out more, Kenny, yet we both know you can't leave anytime you want. But, really, try a cooking show once in a while."

Frank suggested they get writing samples from the four finalists and compare them to the clues in Kenny's puzzle collection. Kenny liked that idea and they spent the next thirty minutes debating how to do this without blowing their cover.

"Blowing our cover? There you go again, Kenny. Keep it up and you'll have me talking like that. Then I'll be a candidate for Gulf Breeze's padded cell wing. Is there one?"

Diary: October 20

Things have settled into a quiet and predictable routine for me. Russell's departure, as upsetting as it's been, actually did wonders at lowering my stress level once I realized that he was gone for good. My inner struggle with accepting the situation at Gulf Breeze versus being "free" like Russell is working itself out. My increasing fogs make running away a nonstarter, not to mention I have family that cares about me.

I was relieved at first that Russell was the likely puzzler. However, I missed the excitement of building my case and solving the mystery. The investigation is back on now, and I'm glad it is. With Frank in the loop, I am motivated to get up each morning and continue my search. Trying to solve a puzzle about puzzles keeps me going. Throw in my own puzzles, Frank's friendship, and flying the drone airplane, life is north of tolerable. Not as full a life as I envisioned a year ago, but the military taught me to adapt to and overcome circumstances. To make do.

I'm not ready to compartmentalize my memory of Russell, nor do I really want to. He's a reminder of the independent spirit we share. For reasons I've already make clear, Russell was compelled to make a drastic change in his lifestyle while I stayed put and am dealing with it in situ. Work in progress, that's me.

To be honest, it wouldn't bother me if it takes a long time to solve the mystery puzzler caper. It keeps me going, thinking, and planning–filling my brain with important thoughts rather than yammering at Sarah to take me home. I'm being selfish again. Someone is asking for my help. It's probably serious. I can't dawdle.

Ha! Frank would love that I said caper.

Chapter 38

Two weeks passed with no additional messages left in the daily newspaper puzzle. Kenny and Frank agreed to take a break from their morning routine. They were both worn out and looked it. Several residents had commented on their reddish eyes of late. Blackjack surmised they were staying up into the wee hours watching porn on TV.

They compared notes while walking the hallways after breakfast. Frank had the duty that morning and wanted to burn off nervous energy fueled by caffeine. He mentioned cutting back on his coffee intake. Kenny said amen to that.

"One of the housekeeping staff is on to me," said Kenny. "She told security I was sitting in the corner of the game room. The security guy flipped on the light and asked if I needed medical attention."

Frank laughed. "Busted, eh? What'd you do when he caught you hiding in the dark with an extra-large coffee?"

"I confessed."

"You what?" Frank said.

"Yep, I told him I had insomnia and was getting up early to wait for the sun to rise."

"What did the security guy say to that?"

"He told me there must be an epidemic going around because housekeeping spotted another male resident doing exactly the same thing."

Frank guffawed and said they're both busted. "Well, we got two weeks of surveillance done anyway. Time to move on to 'plan C.' Too bad we don't have one."

They walked in silence mulling over their next moves. It was Kenny who suggested they directly confront the four mystery puzzler suspects.

"What do you have in mind, Kenny?"

Kenny chewed his lip while he chose his words. "Together, we've spent a lot of time trying to solve this mystery. I have the list down to four people, but you know what? I could be wrong. It might be someone not on the list."

"That has crossed my mind as well," said Frank. "You need to trust your instincts and see it through with the four people before reverting to where every resident of Gulf Breeze is a suspect. Right?"

"You are right. "It's frustrating to feel like we're so close yet can't seal the deal. I want to point blank ask each one if they've been leaving messages in the puzzle. Yes or no. Somebody's in trouble, Frank, and the clock is ticking."

Back on their normal schedules, Kenny and Frank met for breakfast. Frank recognized Kenny's fidgety behavior when he sat down at table 14. He tilted his head and Kenny nodded. Another message was in today's puzzle.

Where RU? was printed in the usual vertical-horizontal way. The "u" ran below the "r" in where. Clever and concise, Frank observed. And a damn good question, he added.

"The mystery puzzler is waiting for you. He or she wonders where you are and what's taking so long," said Frank. "A little creepy if you ask me."

"It's like I'm being stalked," said Kenny. "For God's sake I'm right here. Come and tell me what you want whoever you are!"

Frank cautioned Kenny to lower his voice and take a few deep breaths. Kenny saw the couple at the next table eyeing him curiously. He nodded at them and raised his coffee cup in a mock toast.

"I'm fine, I get agitated when I think about this situation," said Kenny. "Dr. Kim and Sarah would have a cow if they knew how much stress the mystery puzzler was adding to my life."

"Then let's solve it," said Frank. "I like your idea of getting up close and personal with the four people. "It might cause the puzzler to hunker down for a while or forever. However, it might just do what we intend: flush out the puzzler."

Kenny finished his juice and stood to leave. He suggested they let the idea soak for a day and meet up the next morning to discuss how to carry out the direct approach strategy.

"We need to be firm yet sensitive," said Kenny. "Are we up for this?"

"What do you mean *we*? You're the pilot, Kenny. I'm behind you one hundred percent and can help assess your conversations with the puzzler suspects. But as far as confronting them, you need to do this on your own."

Kenny knew this to be true. A two-on-one approach with each of the four could be intimidating and counterproductive. He'd go it alone.

"Hey, I'm Puzzle Man. A superhero in training. If Blackjack was here, he'd say I was a *supper hero* because I love chili dogs, and he'd be right."

Chapter 39

Kenny didn't show up for breakfast or lunch. Frank knew the drill and this time around went directly to Lucy. She had a memory care nurse dispatched to room 258 and the three of them entered together. Frank didn't realize he'd been holding his breath until he exhaled loudly upon seeing his friend sitting up in bed smiling.

No one else smiled, though, when Kenny started to speak. The nurse described his speech as nonsensical; Frank recognized it as plain old babbling. He looked around for empty bottles of alcohol, but there were none. Kenny was in good spirits, and he seemed rested and alert. The two things wrong with the otherwise peaceful setting were the strong odor of urine and Kenny's monotone rambling about his pickup truck.

Sarah arrived within the hour and Dr. Kim rearranged her afternoon schedule so that she could examine Kenny. Dr. Kim consulted with a neurologist from her practice who ordered that Kenny be taken to the hospital for an MRI and other tests. Concern grew throughout the day when Kenny's speech continued to be garbled.

Kenny was returned to Gulf Breeze after hours of testing. Lucy arranged extended nurse coverage and for his meals to be delivered to his room the next three days. Sarah took time off work to be with her father, and Dr. Kim promised to stop by twice a day. Frank raised his hand and said he was available to be a gopher boy as needed. It was all hands on deck in room 258.

Blackjack and Maisey were alarmed to hear that one of their table mates suffered a stroke, which was the diagnosis following the battery of tests and the neurologist's examination. Kenny was confined to his room and connected to monitors while the extent of his stroke was evaluated. After several days of tests and continuous monitoring, the equipment was removed.

"Here's where we are with your father," said Dr. Kim to Sarah. "His stroke caused slight paralysis of facial muscles and the left side of his body, which will make walking more difficult. He can walk with a cane for now. In time, he'll need a walker or wheelchair. And thankfully he's right-handed so he can still do his puzzles and other activities with some effort."

"Is this permanent or will he improve with rehabilitation?" said Sarah.

"Too early to tell. You need to accept that he's likely to always have impaired speech and mobility. Trouble forming words, slurring, stuttering, that kind of thing. The MRI didn't indicate cognitive impairment; the stroke seems to be limited to muscular damage."

Sarah cried softly and wondered if this was the beginning of the end for her father. First the fogs and now the stroke.

"Listen, Sarah, he's 84 with a history of dementia. Now he's had a stroke. With proper care he should live out his life in relative comfort. He'll begin physical therapy soon to keep his mind and body active. Let's give that a chance."

Later, Sarah updated Frank on the information she'd received from Dr. Kim. She thanked him for his support and being instrumental in helping her father accept life at Gulf Breeze.

"Kenny had a tough go of it when Russell was here and when he left," said Frank. "He had to exorcise demons about his perceived loss of independence. I think he's finally come to terms with that... and now he had a stroke. Man."

By day three following the stroke, Kenny had his wits about him. He recalled no details of his incident, only that he was surprised to see so many people in his room. Dr. Kim and Sarah repeatedly explained that he'd had a stroke and the extent of its impact on his body.

With some effort, Kenny could get words out although he'd start and stop often. He told Sarah that he couldn't get used to the sound of his speech–it reminded him of airmen returning to the base after a weekend pass. Hungover and groggy.

"A stroke, eh? The way I feel and sound, my fogs seem like common colds by comparison," he said. "Level with me, Sarah, am I dying?"

"What? No, Dad. Stop that talk. I can't tell if you're serious or trying to be funny. Either way, I don't want to hear it.

You are very much alive and, at the risk of sounding trite, are doing as well as can be expected."

Kenny tried to sneer but suspected that his mouth might already look that way.

"Hand me the mirror. I want to see what others' see. Whoa, more than a little droopy. I never thought of myself as vain, but I think I am."

"Listen, you can talk, walk and do just about everything you did before the stroke. Just slower with more effort," said Sarah. "Work hard in rehabilitation and return to being the Kenny Boone we all know and love."

Sarah was making a valiant effort to maintain her composure. Kenny could tell that she was barely holding on. He told her to go home and rest because he was in good hands. She sensed what he was doing and gave him a long hug before grabbing her purse and car keys. She'd be back tomorrow and would bring him a cheese-and-sausage kolache only if he did his rehab. Kenny agreed. Rehab began in mid-afternoon in the exercise room.

After Sarah left, Kenny pushed himself upright and swung his legs over the edge of the bed. Nurse Lily watched him and said nothing. Years of working with stroke victims taught her the importance of letting patients do for themselves if able. When Lily saw him try to stand, she brought over his cane and stayed close should he need assistance.

"I'm headed to the bathroom," said Kenny, where I'm taking off this damn adult diaper and putting on boxer shorts.

After I do my business, I don't plan on wearing a diaper again. We good, Lily?"

"You pass this test, Mr. Boone, and I'll put in your chart that you no longer need diapers. I'll be right here if you need me."

Kenny leaned heavily on the cane and managed the few steps to the bathroom without toppling over. After a few minutes, Lily heard the toilet flush. In another few minutes Kenny returned to his bed and hung the cane on the headboard in easy reach.

"I did it," he said with a lopsided smile.

"Yes, you did," said Lily with a smile of her own. "I'd say you're officially on the road to recovery."

"Funny you'd say, 'on the road'. What I miss the most about getting old is not driving my pickup truck. Instead of a Chevy Silverado, my vehicle is a cane. The roads I travel are the hallways of Gulf Breeze. Unbelievable."

Chapter 40

Kenny's attempt to compartmentalize his sadness at suffering a stroke was wearing thin. He received accolades for poking fun at his condition–gallows' humor usually elicited chuckles–which put visitors at ease, but only served to suppress his real feelings.

He gave himself credit for getting over the emotional hump regarding Russell and moving on with a positive outlook. Adapting wonderfully, Sarah had exclaimed. *Then I had a stroke that resulted in muscle paralysis, and my world came crashing down,* he pondered.

Kenny's deep thoughts were interrupted when Frank knocked on the door and let himself in.

"Good morning. I brought you a surprise in addition to the daily crossword puzzle," said Frank.

Kenny looked up and saw a grinning Blackjack peering over Frank's shoulder. Blackjack pushed his way in and extended his arm to get a high-five. Kenny made an effort to reciprocate but could only raise his hand slightly.

"Hey, you tried to do the five and that's enough," said Blackjack. "Maisey sends her regards–she wants to know when, not if, you'll be back at table 14."

Kenny glanced at Lily who said that was the doctor's call. If she was a betting person, though, she predicted by early next week.

"Mr. Boone is doing well in rehab," she said. "He complains a lot, but he still puts in the work."

"Hang in there, Puzzle Man, don't let 'em keep you down," said Blackjack. "When Maisey had her big stroke, the docs wanted to keep her drugged and bedridden. I said hell no to that. I was right. She still gets around–with help–and is aware of what's going on."

Kenny thanked Blackjack for the visit and said he looked forward to returning to the dining room. It took effort to get the words out, yet Blackjack was patient and waited for Kenny to finish. He squeezed Kenny's shoulder and said he'd see Kenny around. Frank detected a hitch in Blackjack's voice and thought it might be because Kenny's stroke stirred memories of Maisey's condition.

Lily used Blackjack's exit to excuse herself to see another resident. Frank offered to stay with Kenny while she was gone for about thirty minutes.

Frank moved a chair next to Kenny's bed and told him they needed to talk. Kenny said Frank would have to do most of the talking for obvious reasons.

"Listen, I know my timing may be way off, but I know how you feel about the mystery puzzler. There is a sense of urgency with those notes and you said it yourself that the clock is ticking. What can I do to help?"

Kenny stared at Frank and stated as clearly as he could how Frank could assist.

"I don't want to live out my days being waited on at Gulf Breeze. The fogs are one thing; the stroke is something else altogether. I want to go home. This time I'm dead serious, pardon the expression."

Frank was confused. "The last time you went home to stay you came back here because you wanted to find the mystery puzzler. You're giving up on that? What about the person asking for your help?"

"I'm not giving up. I want you to take over the investigation."

Diary: October 31

I haven't turned out to be much of a friend to Frank. I dumped the mystery puzzler project in his lap. Granted, he offered to help, but it probably never occurred to him that meant taking it over. He's too nice to retract his offer and I'm too focused on finding the mystery puzzler to give him an out.

As far as I can tell, my mind is intact. Except, of course, for the part about my brain not communicating with my face and left side. A pretty big deal, yet manageable if the paralysis doesn't spread. Dr. Kim said my condition should remain stable unless I have another stroke. And my fogs? They're still here, lurking, waiting for their next uninvited visit.

Getting back to Frank and the mystery puzzler. I feel foolish saying this, but I could retain the role of being the brains of this operation (tongue-in-cheek) and Frank could be the sole operative. We'd agree on how he should approach the four puzzler suspects and then report to me after each encounter. Risky, I admit, because they have virtually no relationship with Frank. Acting as my surrogate, though, he might be able to penetrate their privacy veneer enough for us to answer the question 'Are you the one?'.

Then there's the other thing: round two of moving back home. Sarah won't be happy to hear of my plan, nor will Dr. Kim. I already know Frank thinks I've lost my mind. I believe there is more to my medical condition than anyone is letting on. I don't think I'm being lied to, but I do think there is information about my prognosis that they're keeping from me. Good intentions on their part, to be sure, yet I want the truth... all of it. And short of being told the good, bad, and ugly, I'll make up my own mind about my future.

Bottom line for me is I don't believe I suffer from typical post-traumatic stress disorder or PTSD; I have present and future anxieties. That explains a lot about my view of the world and my place in it.

That said, I choose to spend my remaining years at home rather than in an institution. My

Air Force pension and Medicare will pay for in-home care, so there won't be a financial strain on Sarah. There should even be enough cash to finally replace Sarah's carpet–she'll love that.

I've gotten proficient on the computer and smartphone so Frank and I can stay in touch about the mystery puzzler. He can drive over to the house whenever we get tired of communicating via high-tech gadgets. As long as he brings fast-food.

I believe I've thought this plan through objectively. The hard part will be subjective; that is, selling it to my daughter. I'm confident that when Sarah thinks about it, calmly and rationally, she'll be happy to have her old man around the house. I'm counting on it.

So, unless I end up in a wheelchair or worse before moving back home, I'm good to go. Until then, Happy Halloween to all!

Chapter 41

Kenny worked hard in therapy, going above and beyond the exercises prescribed by his therapist. He figured that a key to Sarah agreeing to let him move home was to become functionally mobile. That translated to taking care of personal hygiene on his own for starters. The cane compensated greatly for his diminished left side, and over time he was able to walk fairly steadily.

Kenny soon became a regular sight in the hallways of Gulf Breeze, shuffling along and occasionally emitting a curse word from his Air Force days. His impaired speech made it nearly impossible for the neighbors to know what he was saying, which he thought was a good thing.

"Hey, if you ever get tired of the same old swear words let me know," said Frank, who often joined Kenny on his rehab walks. "I still remember some really good phrases from the Marines. We know how to cuss, believe me."

"It's all coming back to me," said Kenny. "This reminds me of basic training–working up a sweat, getting into shape, the whole thing. Kind of frightening, actually. This time around the finish line is being able to move home. Let's do another lap."

Over iced teas in the bistro, Frank put the screws to Kenny by telling him that going home wasn't a good idea. It didn't work last time, and that was before the stroke. Stay at Gulf Breeze, he pleaded, where Kenny would get top-notch medical care, take pressure off his daughter, fly the drone airplane, and continue working the puzzler mystery onsite.

"You left out one important thing," said Kenny. "If you won't say it, I will. We've become good friends, possibly best friends, and we'd miss each other. That's the way I feel. The friendship would live on with the only difference being I'm not here 24/7."

Frank considered what Kenny told him, but he wasn't convinced.

"And I say *you* left out an important thing," said Frank. "I don't want to run the mystery puzzler investigation. No one's leaving me puzzle messages asking for help. Hell, I don't even do crosswords. This is your mission, not mine."

Kenny saw that it took effort on Frank's part to tell him where he stood on the matter. Kenny also recognized the glimmer of pity in his friend's eyes, a look that had become prevalent at Gulf Breeze. He was getting used to it yet hated it nonetheless.

"No one except Russell understands how I feel about my loss of personal independence... and he's gone. I don't want to die here. I want to go home."

Frank leaned forward and softly scolded Kenny.

"You don't have a monopoly on feelings. Everyone copes with challenges in life and we all deal with them in our own way. I was a Marine and know as much about freedom and independence as you. I choose not to whine about getting old and living at Gulf Breeze."

Kenny was taken aback by Frank's comments. He'd always regarded Frank as a mild-mannered guy, which made his words even more impactful. It was a wake-up call for Kenny, and it also caused him to get defensive.

"Easy for you to say, you have full use of your body and don't sound drunk when you talk," said Kenny. "If you were in my shoes, I bet you'd feel differently."

"True, but being career military, like you, I'd suck it up and move on. That's what we do. What other option is there?"

Kenny shook his head. "The best option I can come up with is to go home and be with my daughter. You have a better one?"

"Best option for you, maybe, but is it best for Sarah? While you consider that, let me remind you that what happened the last time you moved back home. You returned to Gulf Breeze because of the mystery puzzler. That case still is unsolved."

Kenny was speechless. He grabbed his cane and headed for his room. Frank started to follow but was waved off. He watched Kenny shuffle to the elevator and when the door closed behind him, rose to go to his own room. Frank wondered if he'd crossed the line with Kenny, but it had to be said.

Blackjack and Maisey passed by the bistro table that Frank and Kenny had shared; Blackjack paused to comment on the way that Kenny "stormed off."

"Kenny didn't storm off," said Frank. "He has a lot on his mind and is feeling down because of his stroke. We need to give him space to adjust and support him the best we can.

"I know about strokes," said Blackjack, glancing at Maisey in her wheelchair.

Chapter 42

Kenny chose not to talk with Frank for a while about his plan to move home. Instead he had them focus on their approach to confronting Carol, Bert, Yvonne, and Barbara. Frank would take the lead with Kenny as backup. Frank wasn't at all comfortable being "pilot" as he'd much rather remain in the background as "wingman."

They spent several hours reviewing and analyzing Kenny's notes on each of the four. Frank asked lots of questions and by the time they finished he felt he knew enough about them to actually do a decent job. After lunch they did mock interviews with Kenny playing the suspects and Frank asking the tough questions. Kenny skillfully provided vague responses to Frank's questions in order to force him to be firm and direct. Frank eventually got the hang of it.

"I don't know about this, Kenny. If I were one of the four, I'd tell us to butt out."

"You're probably right. I was thinking it might help if I sat in the background while you talked to them. My presence would show support for you and give the appearance that what we're doing is legitimate."

Frank nodded. "Yeah, I like that. You being there might make 'em open up. Let's do it."

Reaction from the four mystery puzzler suspects was unanimous: *What are you talking about?* Bert went so far as to suggest that Frank and his now largely silent partner had gone off their meds or were experimenting with new ones. Frank was deflated, but Kenny, who observed in the background, believed it was time well spent.

"Yeah, the meetings could have been less confrontational," Kenny pointed out. "If they didn't think we were already off our rockers they do now. Did you pick up on Barbara's reaction when you explained the anonymous messages in the crosswords? That hit a nerve."

Frank shook his head. "You should be front and center, not me. This is your project. No one's asking me for help."

Kenny asked Frank if he'd listened to him recently.

"I can barely communicate since I had the damn stroke. You understand me because we spend so much time together. The others? They're trying so hard to make out my garbled words that they don't hear what I'm saying."

Frank agreed, but that didn't mean he had to like it. He paced around Frank's small living room and then sat down again, not sure what to do. After several furtive glances at Kenny, he confessed that the two of them had built a reputation for being nosy conspiracy theorists.

"Think about it," said Frank. "You do crosswords, you get 'help me' messages, you've gone detective and narrowed the mystery puzzler suspects to four after conducting less than forthright interviews. This is your life, not mine."

Kenny stared at his friend. He'd never known him to come on so strongly about anything.

"Well, Frank, don't hold back. Tell me what you really think."

"I apologize, Kenny. Once I started talking it all came out. I went too far. I'm still your wingman."

No one spoke for several minutes. Each was contemplating where to go from there. Finally, Kenny broke the silence with a long sigh.

"You're right, of course," he told Frank. "I've been so focused on solving this mystery that I didn't consider how it might be affecting you. I was wrong to drag you into my world and I'm sorry."

Kenny felt terrible and wanted Frank to leave so he could sulk. Frank would have none of that and insisted they go fly the drone airplane. It took some haggling with the front desk, but when Kenny agreed to use a walker and be accompanied by a nurse's aide, approval was granted. Takeoff from the Gulf Breeze lobby was three o'clock sharp.

Diary: November 19

Frank getting in my face was a much-needed wake-up call. I had become so locked-in on identifying the mystery puzzler that I recruited my friend with little regard to whether he was willing to lend support. He went along with it at first because it sounded interesting and he wanted to help. But after my stroke, his role escalated to lead investigator due to my challenge with speaking clearly. It's turned into a real-time game show at Gulf Breeze, with residents trying to be the first to decipher what I say.

I was preparing to back away from the puzzler situation (I know, again) when another message was left in the daily crossword: "Who cares?" This one deviated from most of the others by not being connected up and down, left to right. The two words were on a single horizontal line of squares with no spaces. A hint of frustration or disdain from the mystery puzzler? Was he or she giving up?

Frank shook his head when I told him about the latest message. He'd become as frustrated as me at making little progress in exposing the identity of the person leaving cryptic messages. He was still onboard with our sleuthing project, although he'd made it clear I was to run the show.

The curious thing about my stroke is that I haven't experienced a fog since I awoke physically impaired. God's will, I suppose, to grant me a reprieve from dementia attacks to make room for slurred speech and reduced use of my left side. If I'd had a say in the matter, I would have chosen to stay with the fogs and do without the stroke. What is it I hear on the news these days?

Oh, yeah, political analysts saying that something or other 'is what it is.'

My latest plan to return home with Sarah is fraught with strong arguments against the move. First, I've tried it before and failed. The lure of finding the mystery puzzler was strong enough to return to Gulf Breeze. And now, my stroke and dementia require special care that I cannot get at home with Sarah. Nor would it be fair to expect her to expand her role as my caretaker. The day is approaching when I'll need help with personal hygiene issues. I would never subject Sarah to what that would involve. So, I can put her mind at rest that I finally accept that the 'right' place for me is right where I am.

So, that brings me back to the mystery puzzler and where Frank and I go from here. It often crosses my mind that the clues are simply a bad joke. A resident could be yanking my chain with the cries for help. If I believed that was the case, I'd be done with it. Frank and I could concentrate on flying the drone airplane and complaining about the food with Blackjack and Maisey.

But my gut tells me the messages are authentic, which means someone at Gulf Breeze needs assistance. He or she chose me and I chose Frank. If two ex-military guys with all the time in the world–knock on wood–can't solve the mystery, then I doubt anyone else here can.

I don't know about Frank, but I never turned down an assignment in 30-plus years in the Air Force. I had a strong sense of duty.

I still do.

Chapter 43

Dr. Kim got right down to business. As usual, she had a full day of seeing patients and was adamant about keeping the meeting at Gulf Breeze on schedule. Kenny, Sarah, and Lucy were seated at the conference table while the doctor stood before a large wall-mounted TV monitor. She ran a PowerPoint presentation by way of a remote control.

"Wow, this high-tech stuff," said Kenny. "I'm impressed as hell." His words were distorted by the stroke, but still understandable. There was no mistaking his mild sarcasm.

"Not so high-tech, Kenny. Pretty standard these days," said Dr. Kim with a smile. "I am pleased to hear you speaking clearer than on my last visit. Speech therapy is helping. That's a good sign."

Dr. Kim talked through slides that covered the timeline of Kenny's fogs, stroke and weeks of physical therapy. There were sufficient charts and graphs to see that she'd done a thorough job of assessing Kenny's situation.

"Bottom line me, doc. I'm just a retired master sergeant with a high school diploma."

Sarah glared at her father and half-apologized for his comment. "That's my dad, a bottom line guy. Unless the data have to do with airplane specifications, he isn't much interested."

Dr. Kim nodded. "I understand. All you need to know about my high-tech slides is that your father's condition is stable... for the time being." She faced Kenny and continued. "The stroke has put a strain on your body as you well know. What we don't know is how this will affect you over time. More physical limitations? Continued dementia episodes? Possibly. We can't predict the future with much certainty."

Kenny broke a moment of silence by asking Lucy her opinion. When she started to protest, he pointed out that she's around elderly people fifty to sixty hours a week, most of whom have medical issues.

"Well, when you put it like that... I've seen many residents with Mr. Boone's challenges over the years. Among those who are able to get along without full-time assistance, the game-changer in terms of quality of life is how they cope with their challenges by keeping busy and reducing stress. Attitude, social activity, support of family and friends, therapy, exercise, and faith all make a positive difference."

Sarah said it was timely for her to mention that Kenny wanted to move home because, as he explained to her, he believed he was dying and didn't want to pass away in an institution.

Dr. Kim looked alarmed but before she could say two words Kenny cut her off.

"Look, I've done some serious thinking since my stroke," said Kenny. "I did say those things to Sarah. But I now realize that as much as I want to be with my daughter, I'm not a very good patient. She has a right to a life that doesn't involve changing my diapers or whatever the future holds. I'm staying at Gulf Breeze."

"I'm pleased to hear this," said Dr. Kim. "I'll spare you my speech about the importance of on-site medical care since we're all on the same page. By the way, what's your reaction to Lucy's comments about quality of life?"

Kenny raised his head and stared at the ceiling. "I don't disagree with anything Lucy said. Different *strokes* for different folks, right? A little bit funny? I'm not big on religion, but I do cherish family and friends. I also believe in keeping busy."

"Mr. Boone and his friend, Frank, are quite the model airplane pilots," Lucy pointed out. "He also is the resident crossword puzzle aficionado. He seems busy to me."

Kenny thought to himself that Lucy was mostly right. She left out the part about the mystery puzzler investigation, which kept him busy (good) but was a major cause of stress (bad). Lucy couldn't be faulted for the omission, though.

Only he, Frank, and the mystery puzzler knew about it.

Chapter 44

Kenny and Frank were enjoying a cup of coffee one morning when Blackjack and Maisey joined them at table 14.

"Did you hear the news?" said Blackjack. "Gulf Breeze now has a new widow. The woman's husband died in their room late last night. Heart attack, I was told. His ticker went out before help arrived."

Life at Gulf Breeze had at least one certainty: it was the end of the road for the majority of residents, at least in an earthly sense. Newcomers quickly became accustomed to the ebb and flow of residents, which explained why it was common to refer to neighbors, acquaintances, friends, table mates and others by first names only. Memory and retention capabilities were limited and declining, making surnames largely extraneous.

"Who was it? Frank said.

Blackjack leaned forward and clasped his hands on the table. He enjoyed being the center of attention especially when he had information others sought.

"My source said it was a man named Herb from the first floor. I don't recognize the name, but I'm sure we've all seen him. His wife is Barbara. Her name doesn't ring a bell either."

Kenny and Frank looked at each other at the same time. Blackjack noticed the reaction to his news and wondered what was going on.

"We know Barbara and Herb," said Kenny, "or I should say *knew* Herb. I was aware he had a heart issue, but not that it was so serious. Did you know, Frank?"

Frank shook his head and said that Herb seemed physically sound to him, adding that Barbara also came across as relatively healthy.

Blackjack dominated the table talk and kept up his lively chatter even as Kenny and Frank excused themselves. The two friends found seats in the game room and sat in silence until another resident put down a jigsaw puzzle piece and departed.

"Well, we didn't see that coming," said Kenny. "Pardon my callousness, but Herb's dying raises the question of whether he was the mystery puzzler. If so, our investigation is over."

Frank raised another question: "How do we determine if Barbara or even Herb was the puzzler other than waiting for more clues? Another clue shows up from the remaining suspects and we're back where we started. We'd have wasted so much time just waiting."

Kenny scratched his head and smacked his knee loudly. "Hold on. Herb wasn't one of the final four suspects, remember? It was Carol, Bert, Yvonne and Barbara. We eliminated Herb weeks ago."

"Maybe we shouldn't have discounted Herb after all," Frank said. "Or we should take a harder look at Barbara. Hell, I don't know."

Kenny went to refill his coffee cup in the dining room and spotted a small crowd around one of the tables. It was Barbara surrounded by friends and well-wishers. He caught her eye and nodded. She was distraught as expected. Kenny made a mental note to pay his respects when her shock of losing Herb wasn't so immediate.

Frank was standing in the lobby when Kenny left the dining room. He asked Kenny what his plan was going forward.

"At the right time, whenever that is, I will call on Barbara, express my condolences, and gently question her about the puzzles. I'll know immediately if I'm out of line and will stop."

"Could be that if Barbara knows anything about the puzzles she might be anxious to talk about it. Get it off her chest, right?"

Kenny conceded that could be the case, even if it was a long shot. Honing in on Barbara and Herb may be the lead they'd been hoping for. Or it was just a long-shot attempt to solve the mystery by taking advantage of a grieving widow.

A win-win or lose-lose proposition. Either way, Kenny saw it as an opportunity that begged exploiting.

Chapter 45

When it was Kenny's turn in the memorial service receiving line at the Gulf Breeze chapel, Barbara squeezed his hand and whispered that she needed to talk with him in private. He said he'd stop by in a few days.

Kenny told Frank about the encounter when they crossed paths in the lobby that afternoon. Frank had missed the service due to a doctor's appointment but paid his respects to Barbara when he saw her in the dining room. Frank was curious about Barbara's request to speak with Kenny. She had not asked him to meet privately, only Kenny.

"I'm actually relieved to be excluded," Frank said, "although I'm really interested to hear how she reacts to your questions about the mystery puzzler. Segueing from condolences to leaving clues in the daily crossword will be quite the challenge."

"I don't know why she wants to meet with me. It's not like I became close friends with Barbara and Herb."

Frank wanted to know details of the memorial service, so Kenny filled him in. He described attendance as sparse. As far as he could tell, the only outsiders were the minister who officiated the service and an elderly man who Kenny later learned was Herb's younger brother. The minister did a passable job of leading the service; it was obvious to Kenny that he did not know Herb. Kenny observed that more Gulf Breeze residents showed up for the buffet lunch than the service itself.

"So, when are you going to talk to her?" said Frank. "There's obviously something on her mind to single you out."

Kenny didn't answer right away. His mind was racing with thoughts of what might lie ahead, perhaps an accusation or confession. He decided to knock on her door after lunch the next day. That would make it two days since the memorial service, which was enough time to both respect her privacy and not appear too anxious. What he needed now was some rigorous PT.

As much as Kenny had come to dread physical therapy, a thrice weekly ass-kicking administered by a young sadist named Nick, the sessions turned out to be opportune times for serious thinking. Since he'd come to grips with living out his life at Gulf Breeze, it freed brain capacity to totally focus on the mystery puzzler.

Nick tried in vain to engage Kenny in conversation while putting him through the paces. Kenny didn't intend to come across as rude, he was simply preoccupied with his upcoming meeting with Barbara.

Successfully blocking Nick's chit-chat was easy. Kenny grunted and groaned while replaying his time with Barbara and Herb. What stood out were Herb's transparent bluster and Barbara's unhappiness. He recalled Barbara's thinly veiled contempt for her husband, most notably his mediocre career and blaming her for being childless. She'd muttered to Kenny when Herb left the room that she was capable of bearing a child–the problem was Herb's chronic low-testosterone level. He'd never admitted it nor did anything about it except to point fingers at Barbara.

"Okay, Mr. Boone, you're done for today," said Nick, tossing Kenny a towel. "Whatever's on your mind must be pretty serious. I've never seen you so focused on rehab."

"Sorry, Nick. You're right about me. I have a lot on my mind. I promise to be friendlier next time."

Kenny stopped in the bistro to get an iced tea to go and spotted Bert and Yvonne walking through the lobby. Their diabetes and arthritis, respectively, hadn't abated judging by the effort it required them to get around. Even with the aid of a walker and cane they struggled. The couple were still on the mystery puzzler suspect list, yet whether they and Carol remained on it would depend on the outcome of his meeting with Barbara.

He glanced out the window on his way to the elevator. Nope, too windy to fly the plane today. Frank would be disappointed.

Chapter 46

When Kenny arrived at room 110 shortly after noon, he was as nervous as a teenager on a first date. He felt like he was intruding on her grieving period.

The door was ajar; he knocked lightly and waited for a reply. Barbara said that for whoever it was to come on in. She was busy packing items in boxes. He assumed it was Herb's personal belongings that she was organizing to give to their children and grandchildren. He blushed when he recalled they had no offspring.

"This a bad time? I can come back."

Barbara gave him a strained smile and replied that it was as good a time as any. She told him to help himself to cookies on the kitchen counter, pointing out that neighbors had brought over enough food to keep her alive for weeks.

"I appreciate the outpouring of thoughtfulness and generosity, but it wasn't necessary," she said. "Last thing I want to do is eat alone in my room. I'll freeze most of the food and save it for when I'm not up for a meal in the dining room."

Kenny thought that was a good idea. He pointed at the boxes and asked if she was moving. She said she was going to stay at Gulf Breeze for the time being but wasn't ruling out the option of finding a new residence.

"My family physician advised me not to make any life-changing decisions for the next six months," said Barbara. "At our age, as you know, a lot can happen in six months. I am reasonably healthy, knock on wood. I don't need a half-year to cope with losing Herb."

Kenny said he recalled the same advice from his family attorney when Rebecca died. He'd moved in with Sarah within two weeks and sold his small home that was walking distance to the Galveston seawall. Being alone was unbearable and fortunately Sarah saw the signs of his depression and quickly took steps to get him out of his now empty home before he could spiral down any further.

Selling his home was a different story. He put it on the market after more than a year and it went quickly. Most of the furnishings were sold via Craig's List and personal effects were boxed and stored in Sarah's garage. Whenever he came to visit his daughter, he spent time resorting the boxes, but rarely threw anything away. Sarah seldom pestered him about getting her garage space back. She knew that what he was doing was therapeutic.

"It's sad to pack up years of memories into cardboard boxes, isn't it?" said Kenny. "What I meant to say was that memories live on in your heart and mind. The things you put into storage are symbolic of a long life together with Herb."

"Storage? All this stuff is going into a dumpster. Now that Herb is gone, I want his crap gone, too."

Kenny was taken aback. He anticipated a grieving widow but what he saw was an angry widow. Barbara wasn't carefully wrapping memorabilia for safekeeping, she was tossing them in boxes until filled, and then securing the boxes with shipping tape. Almost angrily she wrote *TRASH* across the top and sides.

"Barbara, what's going on? Why do you want to talk to me?"

"Look, it's no secret that we knew no one beyond saying hello in the hallways and making small talk at meals. Herb never thought anyone at Gulf Breeze was good enough to be our friends. There was something wrong with everyone except himself. I was miserable with Herb. He was emotionally abusive. I was a willing victim because I stayed with him when I should have left decades ago."

"I don't understand why you're telling me this. I'm not much more than a casual acquaintance."

Barbara pointed out that Kenny at least made an effort to be friendly with Herb and her.

"You came to our room and introduced yourself. You were pleasant and interesting. I had hopes that we'd become friends with you and Frank, another nice man. I could see us playing bridge and drinking wine just like... normal people."

Kenny listened politely and said nothing. He learned from an Air Force officer he served with–and respected–a communication technique in which the major used silence to elicit responses from subordinates who were "called onto the carpet" for disciplinary reasons. The officer would ask questions and then let the airman squirm in awkward silence after replying. Invariably, the poor enlisted man or woman would start talking because the dead-air time was just too uncomfortable. It worked with Barbara.

"I know you wonder why I wanted to see you in private. Please listen carefully and do not interrupt. What I'm going to say is difficult for me."

Barbara stood and began pacing across the small living room. Every few steps she'd wring her hands and look at Kenny. She took a deep breath and repeated what she'd already told Kenny. This time with an occasional sniffle.

"Ours was a loveless relationship. One of my biggest regrets is not having the courage to walk away when I eventually realized his emotional indifference was never going to change. I grew up in a traditional family where the man worked, and the woman stayed home and took care of the house and children. Herb and I had neither."

Barbara recalled that they owned a home early in their marriage, but the bank repossessed it after Herb lost yet another job and couldn't pay the mortgage. They moved to an apartment in another city and started over. It became a recurring theme: Herb got a new job, they relocated to a strange city, rented an apartment, Herb lost the job, and the cycle started over. With bad credit from the house repo and unstable employment history, the prospect of ever owning a home again was a long shot.

"Guess who got the blame?" said Barbara. "You're looking at her. Apparently I wasn't supportive enough and, this one really hurt, I was too matronly and not the right kind of wife for a would-be executive. Herb was a salesman, full of big dreams and big excuses."

"How can you afford Gulf Breeze? This place isn't cheap, and it sounds like Herb struggled with his career."

"Well," she said, "there's a simple explanation for that. Good question, by the way. We're living on inheritance I got from my parents years ago. I invested well and managed to put away a tidy sum of money. Herb never acknowledged where it came from. He convinced himself he was the rain-maker."

Barbara then told Kenny she didn't want to elaborate on the reasons why they didn't have children, only that at one point Herb forbade her from raising the subject any further. He refused to have himself tested at a fertility clinic and was dead-set against adoption. End of story.

"So here I am, an 82-year-old widow and alone for the first time in my life."

Kenny shook his head and said he felt terrible about her situation. Was there anything he could do to help?

Barbara laughed loudly, "You feel terrible? You want to know how I feel? Free! The dark cloud named Herb no longer hovers over me. God forgive me, I'm glad he's gone."

The expression on Kenny's face elicited a snort from Barbara. "Surprised? You've been around long enough to accept that there is such a thing as bad marriages. Mine was more than bad."

Barbara moved next to Kenny and stared at him intently. "Yes, there is something you can do for me. First, I need to know... can you keep a secret?"

Chapter 47

Kenny didn't answer immediately. It was a loaded question, one that he wouldn't answer without additional details.

"That depends," he told Barbara. "I can't promise not to disclose what you tell me if it is illegal, illicit, or is harmful to anyone. Change your mind about me?"

"No, if anything, I trust you more than before. I can tell you're an honorable man. A long career in the military must have instilled clear lines between right and wrong. I'm anxious to get your reaction to what I'm about to tell you"

Kenny leaned forward and clasped his hands in his lap. The suspense had gone on long enough.

"You probably heard that Herb succumbed to a heart attack. True. What you haven't heard, until now, is that when Herb was walking back from the kitchen, he collapsed onto the carpet right in front of me. Food and drink went everywhere. He gasped and turned blue in the face.

"If you assumed that I shrieked and immediately called 9-1-1, you'd be wrong. In Herb's case, dead wrong. I sat and watched him convulse for several minutes until he stopped. He died while I watched. Am I a bad person?"

Kenny stared at Barbara. "You said earlier you're glad he's gone. That statement along with taking no action to save Herb probably wouldn't play well with a judge or jury. I'm no lawyer, but it sounds like negligence. Under the circumstances, though, you were probably in shock and unable to act quickly. Is that a crime? Doubtful."

Barbara stood and went to get herself a glass of water. When she returned, she confessed that the only shock she felt was exultation.

"I was in full control of my emotions and thought of calling for help," she said. "I made a conscious decision to do nothing. For once in our long marriage I was in control and I loved it."

Kenny wondered why she told him how Herb died. *What am I supposed to do with this information?*

Barbara continued. "I watch a lot of police and lawyer shows on TV. In almost all cases, the Crime Scene Investigation or CSI experts pieced together precisely what happened in a homicide. I'm afraid that could happen with me. Would I be better off confessing?"

Kenny shook his head and sighed. He said she was feeling guilty and looking for absolution.

"Look, I'm not a priest and I can't forgive you for what you've done... or didn't do. That's for you to rationalize and live with for the rest of your life. I suggest you chalk it up to trauma and let it go."

Barbara was quiet for several minutes. She finally said that Kenny made good points and that she'd let things play out.

"Good idea," said Kenny. "Perhaps telling me about you and Herb was part of your grieving process. It's never good to keep things bottled up. If you want to talk again, you know where to find me."

He rose and walked to the door, stopping with his hand on the doorknob. Turning around to face Barbara, he hesitated to ask another question. She read his predicament and encouraged him to speak up.

"I apologize for poor timing, but I have to know if you've been leaving messages in the daily newspaper's crossword puzzle. Someone appears to be asking for my help and I don't know who it is."

Barbara winced, giving Kenny the impression that he'd hit a nerve.

"It wasn't me, I can assure you," she said. "But maybe Herb... I just don't know. He was a practical joker and could be petty about people. I can't say he wasn't the one, I just can't confirm that he was. Sorry."

Time will tell, Kenny thought to himself on the way back to his room. He recalled how he suspected Russell was the mystery puzzler right up to the day that another message appeared. And Russell was in Flagstaff. It might have been Herb. All he could do was wait and see, but for how long?

Kenny didn't have long to wait. Five days later another cry for help was left in the crossword puzzle. It was grammatically interesting to say the least. Similar in style to *WhereRU?* If he was right, it was left by one of the three remaining suspects: Bert, Yvonne or Carol. Kenny made a mental note to discuss it with Frank.

Chapter 48

Table 14 was in a jolly mood at breakfast. Kenny had mostly gotten over being self- conscious about his speech impairment from the stroke. His therapy was paying dividends and people were getting used to his new way of talking. The speech therapist had promised that Kenny would see improvement over time, and she was right.

"Puzzle Man, I actually understood you when you ordered an English muffin," said Blackjack. "Your enunciation is getting better, I'll give you credit, but I've always been good at languages–Spanish, French, you name it."

Frank rolled his eyes and muttered that Blackjack invariably turned any subject into one in which he was the center of attention. Maisey winked in agreement.

They chatted about what was on their agendas for the remainder of the day and looked up when Lucy approached their table.

"Good morning, all. It looks like it will be a beautiful day outside, sunny and not too humid," she said, smiling at the foursome. "Mr. Boone, could you stop by my office this morning? I need to talk to you. It won't take long."

"What'd he do, Lucy? Cheat at bingo again?" Blackjack's remark elicited an exaggerated "ha ha" from Frank, and a lopsided smile from Kenny, who said he'd be over in a few minutes.

Kenny rapped lightly on Lucy's office door, noting that for the first time in his memory it was fully closed. She heard her hang up the phone before asking him to come inside.

"So, was it bingo or did someone misunderstand what I said and take offense?"

"Neither, Mr. Boone. Please sit down."

Kenny had a flashback to high school when he and his buddy Perry were caught stuffing potatoes in the dual exhaust tailpipes of a classmate's Ford roadster. It was a common prank and got a lot of laughs when the driver started his vehicle. The pressure of the exhaust blew out the spuds, creating loud popping sounds. The vice principal wasn't amused and put them both on parking lot cleanup duty after school for two weeks.

Lucy was seated at her desk holding a large envelope. The return address was Many Pines Treatment Center in Flagstaff. Inside were two smaller envelopes, one for Lucy and the other for Kenny. She handed Kenny his envelope.

"Before you open yours, I want to tell you about the letter I received from the center," she said. "It informed me that Russell had left unannounced three days ago. Destination unknown. It seems that the treatment wasn't helpful, and he decided to make a getaway while he could still drive."

Kenny stared at Lucy. He was anxious to open his letter but wanted to do so in private. Lucy scanned the rest of her letter and said it had to do with Russell's medical condition. In short, it wasn't good.

"There is concern that Russell lacks the strength to go very far. Worst case is he causes an accident that involves innocent motorists. All we can do is wait to see where he is going and pray he gets there safely."

Lucy looked sympathetically at Kenny. She promised to tell him if she got any further update on Russell's condition or whereabouts. Kenny took his letter to the game room and sat in the corner next to a window. He examined the envelope and hesitated before opening it.

Without reading the letter, he knew Russell's destination: Galveston. His suspicion was confirmed a moment later when he scanned Russell's hybrid print-cursive handwriting. His friend rambled on about the experimental medications he was administered and how they kept him high without doing jack squat at controlling his COPD. A couple of months of being poked, prodded, and doped up was enough for Russell. He got up in the middle of the night, gathered his few belongings, and drove off into the darkness. There was more to the letter.

Kenny, I am heading your way, my friend. Going to take it slow and easy since my stamina isn't worth a damn. The truck's in good shape, though. A hell of a lot better than me. I've stocked up on energy drinks and other nonperishable stuff and will spend the nights at highway rest stops. Hey, they're free and have big, well-lighted bathrooms.

It might take me two weeks to get to Gulf Breeze, give or take, because in addition to taking my time, I'll visit a few tourist hot spots. I've never been to Carlsbad Caverns National Park in New Mexico. 'Now or never' is my mantra.

It would give me great pleasure to arrive in G-Town only to find you've checked out of Gulf Breeze. Not checked out as in passed away; I mean you finally followed your instinct and are somewhere living on your own terms. You know, free, like me. If I find out you've left the old folks' home, I'll hire a teenager to do an Internet web search to track you down. If you're still there, the first beer's on me.

I don't want to get maudlin here, but should something happen during my trek and I don't make it to Galveston, I am leaving my truck and everything in it to you. I got one of those boilerplate wills at the Flagstaff library and had a notary public sign it. Don't get too excited. There is no cash involved; I'm leaving that to my two grandchildren who I never see. I wouldn't be surprised if my son gets his hands on the money and keeps it for himself!

This may be the longest letter I've written in thirty years. It's worn me out so I'm going to sign off. See you when I see you!

Your friend, Russell.

Chapter 49

"How are you feeling, Kenny?" Dr. Kim's familiar voice penetrated his grogginess. He looked around and saw that he was in his own bed. The closed curtains couldn't mask the bright sunlight that poked through. Sarah approached and gave her father a peck on the cheek.

"In case you're wondering, you had another fog episode," she said. "This time it occurred while you were in the game room, reading the letter from your friend, Russell."

Several residents had reported that a man appeared to be sleeping with his eyes open. One elderly gent identified him as "Boone, aka Puzzle Man." Lucy rushed to the game room and found Kenny awake but unresponsive. She called 9-1-1 and Dr. Kim.

"The paramedics got here before me and were still evaluating you when I arrived," said Dr. Kim. "Your vitals were fine considering your history of dementia and the stroke. I knew right away that you'd had another spell and needed rest and fluids."

Dr. Kim reminded them that Kenny had been down this road often and always recovered in a matter of days. In Kenny's case, the fogs had become routine albeit nearly impossible to predict, although they now came more frequently and were longer in duration than six months ago. The trigger, she said, could be just about anything. She excused herself and promised to stop by the next morning. Lucy followed Dr. Kim out the door.

Sarah picked up the letter from Russell and read it again. "Is this what set you off, Dad?"

Kenny thought about her question and softly replied, "I suppose it was. I mean, reading the letter is the last thing I remember until waking up in bed."

Sarah thought aloud that Russell is the man who got her father agitated about moving out of Gulf Breeze and "being free." Since it wasn't a question, Kenny didn't respond. She reread the part of the letter about Russell coming to Gulf Breeze...her expression conveyed irritation.

"Dad, I can tell that hearing from your friend probably caused an episode. I don't know what it is you see in him, but what I see is a man who has filled your head with dreams you simply can't live out. Busting out of here, as you describe it, isn't going to happen. Even you agree that you belong here."

"Yes, yes, I do understand that the stroke changed everything. I can't drive which means I'm stranded at Gulf Breeze. As long as I can get out for chicken fried steak once in a while and spend time with you and Justin away from here, I'll make do."

Sarah was pleased to hear that he'd come to terms with his medical situation. However, news of Russell's imminent arrival had likely caused another fog, which was concerning. Dr. Kim had advised all along about the need for her dad to minimize stress. The reemergence of Russell, however, flew in the face of that advice.

"I'm not going to run away with Russell in case you're worried about that," said Kenny. "You read his letter; he doesn't have long to live. He wants to say goodbye in person and so do I."

Talk turned to Kenny's convalescence and if he'd be well enough for an upcoming home visit with Sarah and Justin. His grandson would be on Christmas break from Texas A&M for three weeks and wanted to hang out in Galveston with family and friends. Justin's high-mileage Honda was in the shop so he was hitching a ride with a college buddy.

"I'd love to come home for R&R; I'll be fine in a few days as always," said Kenny. "I would say 'good as new' but that ain't happening."

As soon as Sarah left, Kenny called Frank's room. He asked his friend to come over as there was something, he wanted to show him.

"The suspense is killing me," said Frank. "Give me a clue."

"Sure, here's your clue: *IBWaiting.*"

Chapter 50

The message light on Sarah's phone recorder was blinking. She'd decided to keep the landline after the police used it to reach her when Kenny ended up on a public bench during his "super fog" of a year ago, the one in which he ditched his truck and walked for miles totally clueless.

Sarah needed to get to work but couldn't resist punching the recorder play button. She listened to Lucy's usually chipper voice, now quiet and somber, say that she was leaving the message for Mr. Boone. Russell had passed away en route to Galveston. There was nothing suspicious about his death, no road rage confrontation or other altercation. He was found slumped in the driver's seat at a rest stop near El Paso. State troopers had his body taken to a city morgue and his truck was impounded.

Lucy paused a moment and then continued. She said a last will and testament was found among his sparse possessions. In it, he had deemed Mr. Boone as the recipient of the truck and its contents. Mr. Boone's address was listed as the Gulf Breeze Penitentiary, Galveston, Texas. The phone number Russell provided was Lucy's direct line.

"I've contacted Russell's son who is arranging for the body to be sent to a funeral home in south Houston for burial," said Lucy. "The truck is another story. It needs to be delivered to Mr. Boone within two weeks or it will be sold at auction and the personal belongings inside will be disposed per Russell's instructions.

"Mr. Boone, I know you're away at a family get-together. I'm sorry to deliver this news on a telephone recorder. I felt it was important to make you aware of Russell as quickly as possible. Please think about his truck and let me know what you want to do when you return to Gulf Breeze. My condolences."

Sarah left a note on the fridge for her father before leaving for work. When Kenny awoke, he listened to the recording twice. No way he could go to El Paso and recover Kenny's truck. The best he could do was to be a trip navigator for someone else who drove. Come to think of it, his map reading skills weren't really needed for the 1,600-miles round trip, what with the availability of Global Positioning System or GPS devices. He had to come up with a plan that would work.

"Sarah, I need to talk to you before Justin gets here tonight. What time will you be home?"

"Dad, I asked you not to call me at work unless there was an emergency, okay? Now what's so urgent?"

Kenny said he had a plan he wanted to run by her, but it could wait until she got home. Justin, she told him, was arriving about nine p.m.

He was pacing the living room when Sarah pulled up just before six. She carried a bucket from KFC and asked Kenny to grab the bag with gravy, potatoes and cole slaw. His mouth was drooling from the aroma and not from his facial paralysis for a change. After dinner Sarah put some food in the warming oven and the rest in the fridge for Justin. Clearly agitated, she pestered him for details about his plan.

"Good Lord, not another plan," she said. "If this involves moving home permanently, I don't want to hear another word."

"No, I'm staying at Gulf Breeze. The plan I have in mind is one that involves me, but in a secondary role. Curious? Let's wait until Justin gets here tonight and I can tell both of you."

Sarah laughed nervously, "Now you've really got me worried!"

Chapter 51

Frank was all in. He readily went along with Kenny's plan and was raring to go.

"How did Sarah and Justin react?"

"Justin was excited, and Sarah was Sarah," said Kenny. "She believes there is more to my plan than I am letting on. I'm certain she thinks that somewhere in the grand scheme is the part where I say I want to return home."

Kenny's plan was straightforward: Frank and Justin fly to El Paso (Kenny pays for tickets and Sarah drops them off at the airport), take Uber to the impound yard, retrieve Russell's truck and drive it to Sarah's house. Justin looked forward to a road trip with Frank; he took a liking to Frank and chatted with him whenever he visited Gulf Breeze. The feeling was mutual.

"The way I see it, you two leave Saturday morning, get to El Paso by noon, and start the drive back by two or so," said Kenny. "You can put in several hours of driving and stay in a motel when you get tired. The second day will be a long drive, but you should be back by late afternoon. How's that sound?"

Frank said it was fine by him as long as Kenny also picked up the tab for the motel, meals and gas. Kenny said that was part of the deal.

"Okay, we're all on the same page," said Kenny. "What I need to do now is prepare a notarized letter authorizing you and Justin to take possession of the truck. I'll attach a copy of my driver's license–I still have one–and call the impound lot to grease the skids before your arrival."

While Frank and Justin were gone, Kenny worked extra hard during his physical therapy sessions. Burning off nervous energy was his goal while waiting for Frank and Justin. He also hung out in the game room doing not only the newspaper crossword puzzle, but a dozen from a puzzle book he'd received for his birthday. He drank a lot of coffee and made frequent trips to the lobby men's room. Blackjack noted Kenny's routine and couldn't help but confront him about it.

"Yo, Puzzle Man, you need to lay off that coffee. Management is going to assess a water usage surcharge for all the flushing you've been doing lately. What's up with you?"

Kenny told Blackjack what Frank and Justin were doing and that he was anxious because he hadn't heard from them since their plane landed in El Paso. Blackjack wondered why Kenny would go to all the trouble to get the truck when he could no longer drive. Kenny said his daughter had asked him the same question and his answer was he didn't know and would figure it out later.

Blackjack followed Kenny from the dining room to the game room going on about how too much caffeine is bad for your nervous system not to mention putting a strain on one's bladder. Kenny paid him no mind and instead concentrated on another crossword puzzle. He glanced at his watch and was about to go find Lucy when she waved at him from the hallway.

"Your grandson is on the phone," she said. You can take the call in my office. Oh, hello, Blackjack. Mr. Boone will be back in a few minutes."

Kenny grabbed the phone and identified himself. Justin said he and Frank acquired the truck after a bit of back-and-forth with a bored state trooper. They ate lunch at a truck stop and were headed to a Best Western motel in Fort Stockton. Justin said that Frank was passing the time on I-10 East by telling stories of his time in the Marines. It was entertaining but smacked of creative fiction.

"How's the truck running? Going to make it to Galveston?"

There was background noise and rustling before Frank took over the phone. "I'm driving and shouldn't be on the phone... pretty sure it's against the law. This truck has serious miles on it yet runs well. Tires are worn and the AC is marginal. We'll call you from Fort Stockton."

The phone went dead. Kenny hung up and went to his room for a nap. He couldn't fall asleep, though. He had enough caffeine in him to watch a Rambo marathon on AMC.

Chapter 52

Frank and Justin parked Russell's Dodge Ram 4x4 pickup truck on Sarah's driveway behind Kenny's Silverado. Justin stretched his legs and went inside the house. Frank drove his vehicle to Gulf Breeze where he fell asleep moments after climbing onto his bed. He knew Kenny was chomping at the bit to talk to him, but his friend would have to wait until nap time was over.

When Sarah came home from work, she stood on the driveway with her hands on her hips. A neighbor walking his dog commented that her place was starting to look like a parking lot for trucks. Sarah smiled thinly and assured him it was only temporary. She called Kenny at Gulf Breeze and advised him that Justin and Frank had arrived safely and the truck was gathering dust as was his own truck. Kenny sensed her irritation and steered the conversation to Astros baseball. That put a quick end to the call.

At breakfast the next morning, Kenny asked Frank for the keys to Russell's truck. Frank had left them with Sarah for an obvious reason–Kenny could no longer drive. He said boxes of papers and other personal effects were stacked in the back seat. There was nothing in the bed of the truck. All in all, not much to show for Russell's 80 years on earth.

Kenny thanked Frank for his role in getting Russell's truck and other belongings from El Paso. He said Justin had mentioned several times what a good guy Frank was and interesting to boot. Frank smiled and said he felt the same way about Justin.

A few hours later, close to noon, Kenny left a phone message for Sarah because he knew that was when she was most likely to call him back. She did and before he could state his business asked if her father had another plan to run by her.

"The only plan I have at the moment is to come home this weekend and spend time with Justin before he goes back to A&M. What do you say?"

"I say that sounds great. I'll pick you up on Friday after work and take you back Sunday afternoon."

"I accept your offer to come and get me, but I decline the return ride to Gulf Breeze. I'm making other arrangements."

Sarah sighed and then started to complain about not one, but two, pickup trucks sitting idle on her property. When she took a breath to continue, he cut her off.

"That's only temporary," he pointed out. "I'm working on a plan for that."

"Goodness, you sound like one of the 2020 presidential candidates!"

Chapter 53

Kenny was reviewing the ten cryptic puzzle messages when Frank sat down beside him. He glanced at the sheet of paper Kenny held and emitted a low whistle.

"Hard at it, I see. I worry about you, Kenny. You're battling dementia and the aftermath of a stroke...you don't need the added weight of the mystery puzzler on your shoulders. Maybe it's time to let it go."

"You stepping down as my wingman, Frank? Want me to go on my own from here on out?"

Frank looked chagrined but held his ground. He said something came up that was distracting him from the normal, slow-pace, and predictable life at Gulf Breeze. When Kenny raised his eyebrows, Frank blushed.

"Do you know of a woman on your floor named Joyce? Widow, late 70s, gray hair?"

"Well that narrows it down to just about every female in this place," said Kenny. "But never mind, what about her?"

"She likes me. I mean she really likes me. "She's been leaving notes under my door and 'coincidentally' showing up at places where I hang out like the TV and workout rooms, dining room, and the patio. I think I'm being stalked."

Kenny laughed and told Frank he may be right, that the woman was stalking him–in a good way.

"My advice to you is to let it play out," said Kenny. "She's probably lonely like most of us at Gulf Breeze and is seeking male companionship. Hey, if a woman was after me I wouldn't complain about it."

Frank shrugged and nodded his head. He agreed that it was a nice problem to have, if indeed it was a problem. He was flattered by the attention, to be sure.

"Man, I feel like I'm back in high school," said Frank. "I was usually shy around girls and I'm sorry to admit I'm the same way 65 years later."

"Let nature take its course, Frank. "No one expects you to marry her. Someone besides me to share coffee, go on walks, or even learn to fly the plane is a good thing. Hell, I'm envious. Now let's talk about the mystery puzzler."

The pattern among the puzzle clues was clear: they smacked of desperation, worry, fear, and that time was running out. Someone, they agreed, needed help, so why didn't he or she articulate their identify so aid could be rendered?

"Perhaps it's a hoax, but it doesn't feel like one," said Kenny. "That means someone, for whatever reason, wants help but not enough to come right out and request it. Why?"

Frank reminded him that they'd been trying to answer that question from the beginning. He viewed the messages as teasing and didn't give them the credence that Kenny thought they deserved.

"You're fixated on the mystery puzzler and I can see why. You're the one being targeted. I'm just the wingman and have the luxury of being openly skeptical. I think we make a good team, kind of a yin and yang thing going on."

"And now you're distracted by a fetching widow named Joyce," said Kenny. "I'd love to be in your shoes right now. Once this mystery is solved, I'll feel like a new man. When that happens, I might ask you if Joyce has any friends."

Frank chuckled. "Whoa, you're moving too fast. I don't really know her... yet. But if that time comes and you're ready, I'll ask Joyce about not just any friends, but a special friend for you."

"If I let you set me up–the Marines bailing out the Air Force–I'll never hear the end of it. But, never say never."

Frank stood at attention. "Oorah!"

Diary: December 7
It's gotten to the point where every day that I awake in bed, cognizant of my surroundings and circumstances, without medical personnel or Sarah hovering over me, is the beginning of a good day.

I'm aware of the increased frequency of my fogs and fear that I could very well end up in a permanent state of fogginess. I pester Dr. Kim about this and she's always noncommittal. As a scientist, she says that my fear could become reality as she'd seen it happen numerous times. On the other hand, as a human, she never underestimates the power of positive thinking, faith and support from others. She said I could worry if that was my nature, or channel that energy into making every minute count.

One of the puzzle messages is "tick tock." I think of that one more than the others because the passage of time is always on my mind. While life at Gulf Breeze is fairly mundane, which is good in many ways at my age and shape, coping with the fogs, stroke, mystery puzzler, and Barbara's confession about Herb are taxing. There's not much I can do about the first two but finding the mystery puzzler and coming to terms with Barbara would go a long way toward helping me concentrate on my health.

Frank is moving on in his life and I have to say I admire the direction he's taking. He's entitled to pursue friendship with Joyce or anyone else for that matter. I should take a page from his playbook and do something like that myself... while I still can. In fact, that's what I'm going to do as soon as I solve the mystery puzzler case. There are a couple of women who are regulars at Jeopardy each weekday that look interesting. I'm reluctant to make any advances because of my speech impairment, so that may be a nonstarter.

First things first: the mystery puzzler and Barbara's personal dilemma. Is she guilty of murdering Herb? Is doing nothing in an emergency grounds for a homicide charge?

How do I get into these messes? How do I get out of them?

Chapter 54

A good part of Justin's last day of semester break was spent on the driveway of his mother's house, working shoulder-to-shoulder with Kenny. The task at hand was to empty and sort the half-dozen boxes in the back seat of Russell's pickup truck.

"You're a good sport, Justin, and I appreciate your help with this and going to El Paso with Frank," said Kenny. "Your mother has about had it with me, I'm afraid. I need to get the two trucks off her property before she blows a gasket."

Justin laughed and slapped Kenny lightly on the back. "Mom's a trouper just like you. I like to think I inherited my ability to work through challenges from both of you."

"I believe you're right about that," said Kenny. "Put your head down, take a deep breath and move forward. I learned that in the Air Force. 'Suck it up, buttercup' is what they instilled in us during basic training. I've followed that directive ever since."

They continued emptying boxes and stacking them in small piles until Sarah called them in for an early dinner. She reminded Justin that he needed to catch his ride back to College Station, and Kenny was due back at Gulf Breeze.

"That reminds me," she said, "you mentioned something about having a plan for your ride tonight that doesn't involve me. Care to enlighten? And don't even think about taking your truck as much as I want it out of my garage."

Kenny smiled and told Sarah they'd be in after placing Russell's belongings on an empty garage shelf. When she reacted unfavorably, he said it was only temporary. Most of it was going to be sent to Russell's son where it belonged.

Dinner was tacos, a side salad and apple crisp. Sarah watched her men wolf it down with a satisfied smile on her face. It gave her great joy to see how close Justin and Kenny had become over the years. The absence of her ex-husband in Justin's life–aside from financial support–was less of an issue now than when her son was a teen. Kenny had done a masterful job during those difficult years by being a strong male role model.

"Well, Dad, what's this plan you've cooked up?"

Kenny sat back and wiped his mouth. "I want Justin to drive me to Gulf Breeze in his vehicle."

"Gramps, you know my car is in the shop and I got a ride with a friend. What are you talking about?"

"I want you to drive me in your new old truck. My Silverado. Want it?"

"Want it? Are you serious? I'd love to have it. That truck is special to me... lots of good memories. Does that mean I can get rid of my Honda? Yes!"

Sarah apologized for suspecting her father of something devious. He had to admit, she pointed out, that some of his other plans had been whoppers. She wondered why he didn't give Russell's truck to Justin and hang onto his own truck for old time's sake.

"I actually thought of doing just that," said Kenny. "But I wanted Justin to have my truck, so it stays in the family. Like an heirloom with wheels."

"I love what I'm hearing, Gramps," said Justin. "What about Russell's truck? It runs fine, but the body could use some TLC."

"I'm donating it to the auto shop program at Galveston's Ball High in Russell's name... he'd be pleased."

Sarah acknowledged that the plan was a win-win-win: Justin got Kenny's truck, the school got Russell's truck, and she got her driveway and most of her garage back.

"There's still the matter of Russell's belongings now sharing shelf space with my gardening tools and clam-digging gear," she said. "I wonder if you have a plan for those?"

Kenny stood and bowed. "Kenny, the planner extraordinaire, does indeed have a plan for those boxes. I'm having them shipped to Russell's son. They belong to him now that his father is gone, even if they weren't close. Sad, isn't it?"

Sarah waved them over for a group hug. She promised that the three of them would always be tight knit. It was the way they rolled.

"C'mon, Gramps, it's time to hit the road," said Justin. "Get your stuff and let's roll. We'll take my truck, what do you say?"

Kenny was deep into the daily crossword puzzle when Joyce sat down next to him. He looked up, startled, and stammered a bit before saying hello. To his ears the word was garbled, and he turned red with embarrassment.

"I think it's about time we met, don't you? I'm Joyce and you're Kenny. How do you do?"

"Of course, I've seen you around Gulf Breeze," said Kenny, putting down his pencil and turning toward her. "Nice to meet you. You're Frank's friend. He's told me about you."

Joyce cocked her head and urged Kenny to go on. He hesitated and wracked his brain for something to say. Frank hadn't been very specific in describing Joyce other than she was not at all bashful.

"He, uh, said you were friendly and outgoing...and attractive." When Joyce stared back at Kenny, he continued. "Frank said he was happy to make a new friend and encouraged me to do the same."

Joyce considered his remarks and smiled. Frank had told her about Kenny's stroke and its effect on his speech. A proud man, and ex-military like Frank, she found him to be blunt and sincere. Joyce liked him immediately.

"You and Frank appear to be cut from the same cloth," said Joyce. "I'm going to enjoy getting to know him and you,

Puzzle Man. You know what? I'm not going to call you by that nickname. Kenny is your name."

"We're going to get along just fine. I can tell already."

Joyce said she and some of her friends noticed that he and Frank spent a fair amount of time talking privately. They had started a poll to guess what was so important that it required such serious conversation. She said the pot was up to 80 dollars and climbing. Any chance Kenny would tell her? Joyce said she'd even split the winnings with him.

"Why don't you ask Frank?"

"I did several times and he plays coy. He said it's top secret and the only one authorized to disclose details is you, Kenny. How about it? Want to make 40 easy bucks?"

Kenny said it was tempting, but his answer was no. He was proud of his friend for staying true to their earlier promise to keep the mystery puzzler case to themselves.

"Okay, have it your way for now. But never underestimate a group of elderly women who have long days to fill. We love challenges and uncovering secrets. We'll talk about this again."

Over lunch, Kenny recapped his visit with Joyce to Frank. Frank confessed that he knew she was going to approach Kenny. It was just a matter of when.

"Man, she didn't waste any time asking you about our so-called covert meetings," said Frank. "I'd bet my life you didn't give her one iota of info about it. Right? That's what I thought. By now she's figuring out that two career military men aren't likely to spill the beans just because they're asked to."

Kenny nodded. "Gotta hand it to her, she knew what she wanted and went after it. I like her chutzpah. She'd have made a good noncommissioned officer in her younger days."

Frank suggested that Joyce could be an asset in the mystery puzzler situation. With her connections at Gulf Breeze and "get 'er done" demeanor, she might be the secret weapon they needed to close the case. Kenny was shaking his head before Frank finished his idea about Joyce.

"No, this stays between you and me at least for the foreseeable future," said Kenny. "I feel that people like Joyce and Blackjack, through their...exuberance...would turn our investigation into kind of a witch hunt. Lots of buzz, speculation, and accusations, I imagine. It could cause the puzzler to withdraw. And then what?"

Frank didn't disagree with Kenny's logic, but he seemed anxious to curry favor with Joyce. He made another run at it with no different result. Kenny wondered aloud if his friend was trying to impress Joyce by intimating that he was in a position of knowledge and would possibly let her in on what he and Kenny were up to. Frank's reaction told Kenny he was correct.

"Your relationship with Joyce is your business, not mine. Let's keep it that way as it pertains to the mystery puzzler," said Kenny. He then asked Frank if he'd talked with Barbara since Herb died. Frank said no and asked why. Kenny replied that there was no special reason. He just wondered.

"Is Barbara still on your suspects list along with Bert, Yvonne, and Carol? What about Herb? I've lost track lately."

"Yes, Barbara is on the list but has slipped a few places," said Kenny. "I asked her point-blank and she said it's not her. She did, however, suggest that it could have been Herb, which was kind of weird. If no further messages are left, that could mean Herb was the puzzler...or not."

"We used the same rationale with Russell, remember? He went to Flagstaff and all was quiet until one day another message appeared. How long do we wait before scratching Herb off the list?"

Kenny glanced up as Blackjack and Maisey sat in their usual seats. Lunch was over, but Blackjack waved over a waitress and requested that she scrounge up a plate of whatever was left from the noon meal. She scurried off to get the food. He turned to Kenny and Frank with a puzzled expression.

"I believe you've both met my good friend, Joyce. She's a force of nature, I assure you. She also is something of a conspiracy theorist and is fixated on whatever you two are up to. I think she's bored and looking for anything to jazz up her daily routine. Unless you tell me otherwise."

"Listen up, Blackjack," said Kenny. "I have nothing to tell you or Joyce. What you see is what you get. Frank and I have a lot in common: we're veterans, widowers, in our 80s, enjoy flying my drone airplane and the list goes on. Beyond that, our lives are not open for scrutiny."

With that, Kenny rose and left the table. Frank followed close behind and quickly caught up with Kenny. He apologized for how Joyce was mucking up the works and adding to Kenny's already elevated stress level. He offered to suspend his budding friendship with Joyce.

"No, Frank, don't do that. We're all grownups here and have the right to pursue happiness. If Joyce brings you happiness, then I'm happy for you. It was just a matter of time before our interviewing residents and spying in the game room got attention. If anything, the growing interest motivates me to put an end to the mystery puzzler business once and for all."

Frank clapped Kenny on the back and walked to his room. Deep in thought, he worried about Kenny's obsession with the puzzles and the strain it was causing on his health. He supported Kenny's goal to end the mystery but had nagging doubts that Kenny would be well enough to to see it to a successful conclusion if it dragged on much longer.

Chapter 56

Kenny had kept a low profile for the past several days. Nothing new, really. No one except Frank and Blackjack seemed to notice his absence at mealtimes and around Gulf Breeze. Since Kenny had ceased making the rounds of residents to conduct his undercover mystery puzzler interrogations, he'd slipped back to his normal persona of keeping mostly to himself. This Kenny was familiar; the brief existence of a gregarious Kenny was becoming a distant memory for many residents.

The rap on the door startled Kenny from a dream about an early career assignment in the Air Force. It was a pleasant dream filled with the pride of keeping combat aircraft prepped for action. He stumbled to the door and opened it slowly. Frank was on the other side holding two cups of coffee and wearing a big grin.

"Making sure you didn't die up here. I'd hate to see a good cup of joe go to waste since I've cut my morning intake to one cup only. You going to let me in or wait until this turns to iced coffee?"

Kenny waved him in and flopped back into his recliner. "No, I'm not dead. When I look in the mirror these days, I look half-dead at least. The day I mistake you for the Ghost of Christmas Future, feel free to call the undertaker."

Frank scanned the apartment and wasn't happy about what he saw. Dirty dishes were piled in the sink, an old t-shirt had been tossed over the TV, and the refrigerator door was ajar. He went to close it and gagged from the foul odor. He peeked inside and removed an object that clearly didn't belong there.

"Kenny, is there some reason why you put your cell phone in the fridge?"

"What? You gotta be kidding me. I was wondering where it was."

Frank studied his friend closely. He noticed that Kenny was slurring his words more than usual. Frank found himself trying to read Kenny's lips, which was something he hadn't needed to do for quite some time.

"Kenny, are you feeling okay? Do you want me to call Sarah or Dr. Kim?"

"No, I'm good, just a little confused lately," said Kenny. "What brings you up to room 582?"

Kenny's room number was 258. Frank thought the juxtaposition of numbers could be nothing more than Kenny being distracted by his visit, or perhaps something more telling. Frank decided to reach out to Lucy as a first step. He tried to use Kenny's phone to make the call, but it had no battery life. Sitting in a fridge for days will do that to a battery, he mused.

"I have an errand to run and will be back shortly," said Frank. "You going to stay here until I get back?"

"How far could I go with the way I walk?"

Frank tracked down Lucy in the exercise room where she was leading a Pilates class. She saw him pacing and called for a break so she could see what had him so nervous.

"I'm certain that Kenny had another dementia episode. He holed up for a couple of days and is acting especially distracted and disoriented," said Frank."

Lucy consulted her iPad and read that the daily nurse visits to Kenny were uneventful. One written comment noted that "Mr. Boone is quiet and sleepy...woke up to take his meds and went right back to sleep."

Frank asked what time of day that visit was made. Lucy scrolled down and replied it was six-thirty in the morning.

"See, something is going on with him. Kenny goes to the game room to work on the daily crossword puzzle between six and six-thirty. I ought to know, I see him there every day. You could set your watch by his routine."

Lucy had heard enough. She had Frank accompany her to the office where she left messages for Sarah and Dr. Kim. She then dispatched a nurse to stay with Kenny until the doctor arrived. Frank said he'd go back to Kenny's room and wait for the others.

Frank hadn't closed Kenny's door completely when he went to locate Lucy, which turned out to be a good move on his part. The smell of something burning greeted him as he pushed his way in. He sized up the situation quickly and took action. Kenny had put a frozen TV dinner–still in the cardboard package–into the oven and set the temperature to 500 degrees.

"Jesus, Kenny, what're you doing?" said Frank, shutting off the oven and placing the smoldering meal under running sink water. Kenny tried to explain how he was hungry and put the food in the microwave to warm it up.

"You used the oven, not the microwave. Plus, you forgot to remove the tray from the box. Go over and sit down and I'll make you a snack. You stay away from the oven from now on."

Frank glanced at his watch while preparing a plate of cold cuts and fruit. He carried it across the living room only to find that Kenny had fallen asleep in his chair. Frank put plastic wrap over the plate and set it in the refrigerator.

Exhausted and worried, Frank sat down on the sofa next to Kenny and waited for help to arrive. Soon both he and Kenny were snoring.

Chapter 57

"I'm going to tell you straight out that I'm concerned about your father," said Dr. Kim, after examining Kenny. She had taken Sarah by the arm and led her into the hallway for privacy. "A decision has to be made regarding his future care and treatment. I'm sorry it's come to this, but not surprised."

Dr. Kim explained that she recommended a more comprehensive level of memory care than Kenny currently received. She wanted to move him to a room in a dedicated memory care area at Gulf Breeze where, among other services, a nurse was on duty 24/7, in-room meals were provided, and there were customized health and social programs. The oven would be disconnected, and the space heater removed.

"I know what my father would call this," said Sarah. "A prison without bars. But I don't suppose we have any choice, do we?"

"Yes, you could transfer him to a facility that only serves Alzheimer and dementia patients. There are two reputable ones in Houston. Is that something you'd consider?"

Sarah leaned against the hallway wall, clearly dejected. Her vote was to leave Kenny at Gulf Breeze unless Dr. Kim had medical objections. She believed that the risk of him incurring a setback brought on by new surroundings was very real–an emotional roll of the dice with poor odds.

Dr. Kim concurred and pointed out that Kenny's strong friendship with Frank was a huge plus in helping him cope with his declining condition. She locked eyes with Sarah, who nodded slightly.

"Not to mention that moving him to a Houston memory care facility would put a strain on us because of the driving time to and from from Galveston. So, we're in agreement that your father will get the care he needs right here at Gulf Breeze."

Back in Kenny's room, Dr. Kim told Kenny that he was being moved to a similar room on the first floor. His furniture and belongings would be moved and set up just like in room 258. Sarah recognized the anguish forming on his face and stepped in to provide moral support.

"I realize that you've grown accustomed to this room and think of it as home, but the alternative is to move you to a strange place and start over. You understand what's happening here, don't you?"

Kenny raised his head and regarded his daughter. "Yes, I know that my fogs are more frequent and unpredictable. I don't want to leave here unless it's to move to my real home... with you."

He paused and lowered his head. When he raised it again, a tear rolled down his cheek. "Do what you need to do. Will you tell Frank? Give him my new room number?"

"Daddy, you sound like you're saying good-bye, that this is the end of the line. You're going to change rooms and get more TLC from the staff at Gulf Breeze. You can still go to the dining room, game room, TV room, and hang out with Frank in the bistro."

"Can I still fly my airplane and do crossword puzzles?"

Sarah and Dr. Kim must have been reading each other's minds for they spoke the same word in enthusiastic unison.

"Absolutely!"

Chapter 58

"They didn't waste any time putting you in room 103," said Frank. "Somebody just die and the room become available?"

Kenny attempted a smile worthy of his friend's effort to lighten the moment. What came across was a crooked mouth formation that Frank had gotten used to since Kenny's stroke.

 "Glad you found me. I wonder who'd answer the door in 258 if you'd gone there." said Kenny.

Frank admitted that he'd just come from room 258 where two husky fellows were moving in furniture. He didn't see anyone who might have been the new tenants, however. He asked one of the movers about the person or people moving in, but the fellow had no idea.

"Doesn't matter to me," said Kenny. "This room is the same as my old room, just one floor lower. I was kind of upset at first, but I'm okay now. I'm a short limp from the main areas of Gulf Breeze. Less elevator time."

Frank asked about Kenny's ability and willingness to eat meals at table 14 with the old gang. Even if it were only once in a while, he said, they'd love to keep their foursome intact as much as possible. In any event, Frank got assurance from Lucy that Kenny's place would not go to anyone else.

Kenny was touched that his meal mates felt that way about him. He promised himself to work harder in physical therapy so that he could regain some of the losses he'd suffered the past year. There was no kidding himself, though.

Kenny might learn to walk with less of a hitch in his giddy up, yet no amount of rehab could fully restore his steadily declining cognitive abilities. Dr. Kim was steadfast in her advice to reduce stress and increase social interaction. The stress thing was a tricky one, he knew. As long as the mystery puzzler continued to leave appeals for help, his stress level would stay elevated. No way he could let go of it until it came to a conclusion.

"Frank, I've been rethinking Joyce's offer to get involved with our business. Maybe there's a way to take advantage of her... enthusiasm. I'm on the bench for a while, you want to back out, so why not recruit a new mystery puzzler investigator? Something to think about."

Frank's mouth dropped open in surprise. He told Kenny that was the last thing he expected to hear today. In fact, he was reluctant to talk about Joyce at all because he suspected Kenny got a mixed impression from his first meeting with her.

"Before we discuss what Joyce could do for us, I want to get your opinion on something that's been bothering me," said Frank. "You mind being my sounding board on a personal matter?"

When Kenny shrugged his shoulders, Frank took it as a sign to proceed. He said that one of the web sites he subscribed to, *Retirement Living Clearinghouse*, called attention to common scams targeting senior citizens. In the top five was one titled *marriage schemes*. Referring to his scribbled notes, it went like this:

Single, retired military men who live in nursing homes or other senior residences are particularly vulnerable to marriage scams. At one facility, presumably not Gulf Breeze, widows and even single nurses were known to marry isolated, vulnerable veterans for their pensions, benefits, property, vehicles, etc. Some wives even lived in their own homes away from their elderly veteran husbands.

"What's your point, Frank? You think Joyce is after your retired gunnery sergeant's pension and vehicle? No offense, but she seems too high society to target anyone less than a light colonel."

"I know, I know. I sound paranoid, don't I? Still, it does happen enough that an article was written warning guys like us to be aware."

Kenny said he couldn't help Frank with his personal dilemma; he'd have to work that out on his own. However, they needed to collaborate if Joyce was going to be brought into the investigative fold. Set solid ground rules, for starters.

They discussed the role they wanted Joyce to take to get close to Bert, Yvonne, Carol, and Barbara. The idea was for her to win the trust of the suspects in hopes of uncovering the actual mystery puzzler. At no time was she to divulge her mission, but rather was to nibble around the edges to elicit a clue that would yield results.

"I like the sound of that and think it's worth a shot if we get Joyce to agree not to talk about this with her friends, only you and me," said Frank. "I'd hate for the Gulf Breeze rumor mill to get hold of the mystery puzzler situation."

"'Loose lips' are my main concern," said Kenny. "If there's anything that could cause the puzzler to take even a lower profile it'd be people talking and speculating publicly. People love conspiracy theories. Can we trust Joyce?"

Frank wasn't sure because he didn't know her very well. He said they'd have to get a firm commitment from Joyce to keep the matter confidential in order to maintain its integrity. If they had any doubts about her ability to be a team player, she wouldn't be included. It was a risk, he acknowledged. That was the understatement of the month, according to Kenny.

"So that's it, Joyce. What do you think?"

Joyce listened politely while Kenny finished outlining his proposal. Frank had chimed in just enough to demonstrate that he was a partner with Kenny. He also served as an interpreter when he could tell she had trouble understanding a few of his friend's garbled words.

"Wow, that's quite a story," she said. "Am I allowed to ask questions now?" Without waiting for a response, she fired away. "Who are the 'suspects' as you call them? Do they have any idea what you're up to? Is Gulf Breeze administration aware of the puzzle clues? I'm sure they'd be concerned that one of their residents is calling for help."

Kenny said that the only people on earth who knew about the puzzle messages were the three of them–four if you counted the puzzler–and he wanted it to stay that way.

"We took a chance telling you about this," said Kenny. "Frank vouched for you and I trust Frank. So, here we are. Do you want to help us? Can you keep it confidential?"

Joyce raised her palm. "Yes, I want to help, and I promise not to tell a soul, although the women I'm close to here are pretty darned good at unraveling mysteries. This one is a doozy so I'll be extra careful not to say anything to get them guessing."

Kenny and Frank expressed their acceptance of Joyce's vow for nondisclosure and they shook hands all around. Frank told her the names of the four suspects and asked her not to keep written records of her encounters with them. Everything from here on out would be done verbally and out of earshot of others.

Joyce gazed at Frank and winked. She giggled when he squirmed and turned red.

"I can see the need for Frank and I to meet often to discuss my findings. Private meetings, just the two of us, right Frank?"

Frank stammered. "Well, I, uh guess so. You have a way of making me nervous, you realize that Joyce?"

She laughed and Kenny managed a lop-sided smile.

"I have to admit I'm enjoying Frank's discomfort," said Kenny. "A career jarhead, combat veteran who I believe is smitten with you, Miss Joyce."

"No reason we can't mix business and pleasure," said Joyce. "Which reminds me, Kenny. I know someone you've got to meet. A good friend of mine. Say when and I'll reserve a table for four in the bistro."

"Please don't play matchmaker for me," said Kenny. "Have you looked at me lately? Heard the way I talk?"

"I see a kind man and I hear an intelligent, but lonely man," said Joyce. "You're a good friend to Frank. That's a winner in my book."

"Don't put me on a pedestal," said Kenny, obviously touched by Joyce's remark. "I'm just Puzzle Man."

Diary: December 31

It's taking me forever to type this entry. My left hand isn't what it used to be since the stroke. Excuse the typos and all the Liquid Paper it takes to get through this.

I settled into room 103 without any fanfare. Same layout as 258 so adjusting to it has been no big deal. Ground-level view is not as nice as second floor. Instead of looking down on cars in the parking lot, I now have a straight-on view of license plates. I keep the curtains pulled most of the time so ... .

My secret has taken on a life of its own, it seems. First me, then Frank, and now a feisty woman named Joyce is involved with trying to identify the mystery puzzler. As the circle widens so, too, does the very real chance that the whole thing will unravel with the worst possible outcome: failure to find the puzzler in time or at all.

I've been reorganizing my notes on the mystery puzzler. Not that they really needed to be sorted, labeled, edited or revised beyond what I've already done, it's just a way to keep me engaged in the investigative process. I don't intend to take a backseat indefinitely. When I'm able, I'll resume my role as lead investigator with Frank as wingman and Joyce as... wingwoman? I hope Joyce works out for us. Three months ago I'd have never considered bringing in an outsider like her. Funny how ongoing fogs and a stroke can change things.

I was alarmed when Dr. Kim told me that Frank came by my old room and discovered that I'd put a TV dinner, still in the carton, into a hot oven. That was not like me at all. I am always so careful around appliances and equipment that use electricity or combustible fuels. I was a chief airplane mechanic and look what I did. Lucky I haven't hurt myself, or anyone else. A few more fogs and who knows what havoc I can wreak?

These latest experiences of the fog and forced move got my attention. Just when I had put together a string of months in which I had accepted my fate, I've reverted to thoughts of returning home again. Gulf Breeze is where I reside, it's not really home. I think a lot about home these days, about Rebecca, Sarah and Justin. I also contemplate Russell's last days: alone on the road, estranged from his son, literally dying in his truck on a road trip to visit me in Galveston. I have this image of Russell slumped over the steering wheel just outside El Paso. Dead as hell. Jesus.

As always, I'm torn between wanting to live out my time at home versus at Gulf Breeze or some similar facility. Lucy and the other staffers frown on anyone referring to it as a facility. They're right, of course. Who wants to live in a facility?

I'm going to make an effort to eat dinner each evening at table 14. Dr. Kim and Sarah were happy to hear me make that pledge because of their desire for me to remain socially active. That's all well and good, I just need to get out of this room before I go crazy. At least for an hour or so I can escape the constant barrage of nurses checking on me, taking my pulse, making sure I swallow my meds.

Tomorrow's a new day. It'll be just like yesterday and today, no doubt. I'm going to get Frank to take me across the street to fly my plane.

It's time I promoted him to pilot. Happy New Year, buddy.

Chapter 59

Joyce had been busy. Kenny couldn't help but notice the flurry of activity that she generated when bustling about Gulf Breeze. Knowing what she was up to, he found himself amused and curious–she certainly knew how to work a room. In his younger days Joyce would've been the first person he'd invited to a party if he wanted to encourage mingling.

Today, she spotted Kenny working on a crossword puzzle in the game room and hustled over from the main hallway. Without a "good morning" or "got a minute?" she pulled up a chair and started talking almost breathlessly. Kenny told her to slow down because his ears couldn't keep up with her mouth.

"I decided not to jump right into the mystery puzzler case. Instead I'm buddying up to the residents who I know to be social, outgoing and connected. People who get around and hear things. You know, people like me."

Kenny thought it made sense for Joyce to take a measured approach to her task. The bull in the china shop tactic likely wouldn't play well among the majority of residents. Joyce was targeting people like herself who thrived on social buzz. Smart.

"I hope that however you're doing this you use tact and restraint," said Kenny. "Remember you are not to take any action should you uncover what we referred to in the Air Force as 'actionable intelligence.'"

"For the hundredth time I understand, General. I report back to you and Frank, that's it. Clearly you don't trust me...yet. Frank may have told you that I had a long and successful career in corporate public relations. I know all about building trust and credibility, as well as effective messaging, active listening, and persuasion. If anyone of the three of us has the tools to find the mystery puzzler, it's me."

With a bit of a flounce, Joyce rose and strode with a purpose to the bistro where she saw one of her buddies standing in line to get a coffee. Even from the game room Kenny could hear Joyce's sunny greeting and invitation for her buddy to join her for coffee on the patio. Joyce was a piece of work, Kenny thought to himself. Frank had his hands full with this one.

"Keep the nose up or you'll put her in a tailspin," said Kenny to Frank, who was doing a respectable job of flying the drone airplane. "Don't look at me while you're flying. Concentrate on what you're doing."

"Easy for you to say, you're an ace at flying this thing," said Frank. "It doesn't help to have you critiquing my every movement. I think I'm doing pretty well, don't you think?"

Kenny conceded that Frank had the makings of a darned good pilot. A few more private lessons and he'd earn his wings from Kenny. Frank flew in silence while Kenny watched approvingly. He put the plane through a regimen of dives, loops, and soft landings. Finally he shut down the controls and turned to Kenny.

"We're going to talk about the mystery puzzler, aren't we? We always do sooner or later. It's just you, me, and the nurse's aide who is busy reading a paperback book. It's called *Quest for Closure*. Never heard of it."

Kenny wondered aloud if Joyce had recently updated Frank; she obviously was more likely to brief Frank on her progress than himself. When Kenny referred to him as her "boyfriend" he scoffed. He didn't deny it, though.

"Joyce told me yesterday that she'd chatted with Yvonne and Carol. Mostly small talk, nothing substantive. She plans to do the same with Bert and Barbara when the opportunities present themselves. What she'll do after that I haven't a clue."

Kenny was relieved that Joyce hadn't yet talked with Barbara. He asked Frank to subtlety mention to Joyce that she was to tread lightly when it came to Barbara. He knew her to still be in a fragile emotional state after the circumstances surrounding the death of Herb. Frank was aware of Kenny's concern for Barbara, but could tell there was more that Kenny hadn't shared with him.

"I'll let Joyce know when I see her later today," said Frank. "Do you plan on filling me in on Barbara?" When Kenny's reply was silence, Frank didn't push it. "I sense there is a dark secret at work here. I respect her privacy and your decision not to divulge that secret."

"I made a promise to Barbara and I keep my promises," said Kenny. "If the situation changes to the point where it's okay to tell you, believe me I will. I could use your advice on what to do about it. It's a doozy."

They parted ways in the Gulf Breeze lobby. Kenny got on the elevator but quickly shoved his arm into the door opening before it could shut. The door reopened and he made his way to room 103 instead of 258. Force of habit. Back in his recliner, Kenny stared out the window at the parked cars, reciting license plate numbers until he could no longer keep his eyes open.

Chapter 60

It'd been nearly a week since Kenny joined the others for breakfast at table 14. All but Frank were surprised to see him. Kenny told him the night before he planned to eat with them if he felt up to it. In anticipation of seeing his friend, Frank had bundled a small stack of daily newspaper sections that contained the crossword puzzle. Every few days he delivered the papers to Kenny in his room. Today he would make the handoff over oatmeal and rye toast.

"Still living up to your nickname, eh Puzzle Man? People here collect stamps, paint by number, quilt, and even do jigsaw puzzles to kill time," Blackjack said. "But you hunker down alone and do crossword puzzles. You're not what I'd describe as a social butterfly."

Kenny concentrated on spreading jam onto his toast. Frank couldn't let Blackjack's jab go unchallenged.

"Your hobby seems to be criticizing others. I like you, Blackjack, we all do. But good Lord you take your shtick too far sometimes. You need to filter your comments with empathy."

Blackjack's expression went from surprise to anger to resignation. He took a sip of juice and glanced at Maisey before locking eyes with Frank.

"Whoa, where'd that come from, Frank? I must have struck a nerve with you. Funny, you're the one who took offense and Puzzle Man said nothing. But, your point is well taken. I meant no harm. My comment was meant to be nothing more than an observation, one that I could have phrased better."

Kenny spoke up. "I had a young second lieutenant right out of ROTC at Lackland Air Force Base. He was always quick to criticize and demean. I think he was compensating for his insecurity by making snide remarks to airmen who had more experience than he did. Very unpleasant."

Frank said he knew the type from his career in the Marines. He pointed out that those officers either got their act together or paid the consequences with poor fitness ratings. That usually led to slow promotions and undesirable assignments.

"Well, this isn't the military, this is a senior living community," said Blackjack. "Maisey and I aren't going anywhere until Judgment Day. How does this sound? I will try to temper my comments if you two develop a thicker skin. We'll meet in the middle, still friends."

With breakfast over, the foursome got up to go their separate ways. Kenny couldn't resist a parting shot as he tucked the newspapers under his arm and turned to leave.

"Blackjack, I accept your proposition. Now I have one for you: Get a book of crossword puzzles. They come in large print for us elders. You get stuck on clues and I'll help you out. It'll help expand your vocabulary. I promise. And the way you like to talk–it's a perfect match."

Kenny carried the puzzles into the game room and got to work. Forty minutes later he called it quits due to fatigue. As he put the newspaper sections into a neat pile, his eye caught something amiss. One of the puzzles he hadn't yet gotten to was partially completed. His chest tightened when he read the single entry.

3 is a crowd.

Chapter 61

"Well," said Frank, "this latest clue eliminates Herb as a suspect. We're still left with a final four of Bert, Yvonne, Carol, and Barbara. Not sure where we go from here."

Kenny said there was another issue they had to consider: the mystery puzzler knew that three people were trying to track him or her down. The message said it all: three's a crowd. Who talked? Both Kenny and Frank turned to Joyce and instead of withering under their glares, she didn't waver one iota.

"Don't look at me, I haven't told anyone what I'm up to," she said. "Maybe one of you guys let it slip out at your dining table. We all know that Blackjack doesn't miss much."

Frank and Kenny turned their gazes from Joyce to each other.

"No way did either one of us talk about the mystery puzzler," said Kenny. So if we didn't tell and you didn't tell, what happened?"

They kicked around several "what ifs" but none of them seemed like a slam-dunk winner–possible, not probable. It was Joyce who suggested that the earlier meetings that Kenny and then Kenny and Frank had with the "residents of interest", followed by Joyce's involvement, aroused suspicion to the point that one of them started asking questions. She added that her friends had noticed how often she spent time with the two men and were quite curious as to why.

Frank nodded. "She's right. Put all that together and we are attracting attention. Someone as secretive and clever as the mystery puzzler could figure out that Kenny has partners. Guess we haven't been as covert as we thought."

Kenny wondered what was going to happen now that the mystery puzzler was aware of their investigative efforts. Did it make any sense for the puzzler to go dormant?

"Think about it. This person, if legitimately in trouble, has been reaching out to me for months," said Kenny. "Apparently asking for my help, whatever that means. But instead of approaching me directly, the puzzler has been coy by leaving me eleven clues."

Frank jumped in when Kenny paused to take a long breath. "So why not come forward to you and put an end to growing speculation about our investigation? Unless, unless this whole thing is a farce. A resident who is bored and having fun playing us for fools?"

"What has bothered me since I got involved is wondering what the cries for help are all about," said Joyce. "If it's a life or death situation then leaving clues in the daily newspaper is definitely not the way to go. And why you, Kenny? Because your reputation as Puzzle Man appeals to the puzzler?"

Kenny didn't disagree with the points made by Frank and Joyce. He was torn between calling the situation a hoax and dropping it or continuing to take it seriously and completing the investigation. He feared that the latest clue indicated discomfort with three residents rather than only Kenny in the know.

"Here's where I am," said Kenny. "Because of the tone of the messages, I'm reluctant to write this off as some kind of sick joke. I'd feel terrible if I did so and the outcome was tragic. Unless and until it's proven otherwise, I'll regard this as authentic. You both still in?"

Frank noted Joyce's nod and assured him they were still in. Kenny looked pleased and relieved.

"As your friend, I have to tell you that I'm worried about you, Kenny. Dr. Kim and Sarah would back me up on this... you should concentrate on getting better, not chasing down the mystery puzzler. There could come a day when you cannot be involved with the investigation any longer. Where would that leave Joyce and me?"

Kenny said he'd go as long as he was able. Beyond that, it was up to the two of them to decide what to do.

"The clock is ticking for the puzzler and me," said Kenny. "That makes it doubly critical to resolve the mystery as quickly as possible. We just need a break. Maybe the fact that the puzzler knows that the three of are working together will spur him or her to step forward."

Joyce pointed out that still left the other part of the problem—what to do about rumors of their task spreading through Gulf Breeze. She said that during her PR career there was a common expression they followed: never let a good crisis go to waste.

A crisis? Is that what's brewing? Kenny and Frank were familiar with crises. The term crisis wasn't used lightly in the military. Hearing Joyce refer to the mystery puzzler and the

Gulf Breeze rumor mill as a crisis was disturbing. He hoped the crisis stage wouldn't be attained and would gladly settle for a "big problem" instead.

"What do we do next?" said Frank, seeing the look of despair on Kenny's face.

"I don't know, Frank. But whatever it is we need to do, do it quickly for the sake of the mystery puzzler and... me."

Chapter 62

It was debatable whether the mystery puzzler situation was indeed an emerging crisis or still at the problem level. Regardless, it was big stuff for the management of Gulf Breeze. The summonses were delivered three weeks later.

"I called you here today because it has come to our attention that you're involved in something that is raising concern among the residents," said Karen, the administrator of Gulf Breeze. By "our" she meant Lucy, who was seated at the end of Karen's desk facing Kenny, Frank, and Joyce.

Kenny said he knew what she was talking about. The other two squirmed in their seats, not unlike being called into the principal's office in junior high school. "Scold me if you must–I recruited Frank and Joyce to help me."

"I'm not sure that scold is the right word," said Karen. "Before discussing semantics, I want you to tell me what you're up to. Lucy has already briefed me on what she knows, so let's compare notes."

Kenny pulled a sheet of paper from his pocket and set it before Karen and Lucy. It listed the eleven clues left for him in the daily newspaper dating to shortly after his arrival at Gulf Breeze. He'd put spaces between the words for clarity and watched them react as they read the clues.

help me

time is near

getting late

don't leave me

i'm desperate

tick tock

why me?

where ru?

who cares?

i b waiting

3 is a crowd

"Wow, I'm flabbergasted," said Karen. "You said this has been going on for about a year? Why didn't you notify the staff? We have a responsibility to protect you and every other resident at Gulf Breeze."

Kenny admitted that in retrospect he probably should have done just that. He said if there was any finger pointing to be done, to aim it his way.

"I was hopeful that eventually the mystery puzzler, as I dubbed this person, would come forward. Keeping the clues quiet was intended to build confidence and trust. However, the clues kept coming and I didn't make any progress toward identifying the puzzler. That's why I brought in Frank and Joyce.

"Time passed and through a process of elimination, we got the list of likely suspects down to four people. We've devoted a lot of energy to get to this point. The hell of it is the mystery puzzler may not even be one of the four. In that case we've wasted our time."

Karen and Lucy were enthralled with Kenny's story. Lucy made the point that fortunately it wasn't too late to help the resident in question; as long as the clues kept coming the window was open to provide assistance, she said.

Frank reminded the administrators of Kenny's medical challenges and the toll the mystery puzzler has taken on his overall health.

"Kenny's deeply concerned about this person and frustrated that he or she is still unknown to us. He is supposed to reduce stress, but that's been impossible."

Frank added that he and Joyce have shared some of the load of meeting with residents to extract information that would point them in the right direction.

"Make no mistake, Kenny is carrying the bulk of responsibility and worry. The mystery puzzler chose him. We're just trying to help."

Karen asked Joyce how she got involved and if she'd like to contribute to the discussion. Joyce smiled. "You're not used to seeing me not chatting a mile a minute, are you? Frank and I are friends and I noticed how often he and Kenny huddled in a corner in serious discussion. Solving the woes of the world, I figured.

"Well, being a former communications pro, I saw the signs of something juicy brewing and wanted to be part of it. It took some doing, but eventually Kenny and Frank opened up. They realized they needed help finding the mystery puz-zler. So here I am."

Karen regarded Joyce and then looked at Frank and Kenny, "I believe your hearts are in the right places and I com-mend you for your integrity. There are three things in play here that have my full attention: Mr. Boone's health, the mys-tery puzzler, and managing rumors among the residents about what you're up to. It's time to take a strategic approach to addressing all three."

Kenny wondered what she had in mind and if his ad hoc investigative team was being benched. Karen said she and Lucy needed to hammer out details, but for the time being he, Frank, and Joyce were to cease pursuing the identity of the mystery puzzler. No more veiled conversations with the so-called final four until further notice, she said. Kenny was to focus on reducing stress and taking better care of himself. Backing off from the investigation would be a smart step in the right direction.

"So, we're done? That's it?" said Kenny. "I'm not sure I can do that."

"Let's call it a time out. You, Frank, and Joyce should share your notes and thoughts with Lucy and I. Working to-gether, we can decide how to proceed."

Karen then asked if Joyce would be willing to help de-velop a communications plan to manage the Gulf Breeze ru-mor mill. Joyce beamed her acceptance.

"Okay, then, we're all in agreement?" said Karen, addressing Kenny when asking the question. He concurred so she wrapped up the meeting.

"This has been, er, enlightening. "Thanks to each of you for your hard work coming to the assistance of another resident. This is a close community that is known for looking after its own. You two gentleman know all about having each other's backs.

"Lucy will contact you with dates for us to get together. Let's keep the details of this and future meetings confidential. I've no doubt that a new iteration of rumors will begin when you're seen coming from my office."

Joyce went to watch a game show and Kenny took Frank's elbow and led him to the patio.

"What do you think, Kenny, you okay with the way this is turning out?"

"Yeah, it had gotten to be a big burden to carry around," said Kenny. "We can use the infusion of fresh ideas as well as the added resources of Gulf Breeze staffers."

Frank said he thought Karen's three-point strategy was right on.

"She reminded me of the public affairs officers I occasionally crossed paths with on active duty," said Kenny. "Smart, articulate, and big picture folks. I like her."

Frank raised his head to take in the incoming clouds. Another front was forecasted. "Maybe with the extra help we'll finally solve this mystery."

"Remind me to tell you about another mystery that's bothering me. It has to do with Barbara and the death of her husband, Herb. A story for another day."

Chapter 63

The word-of-mouth network at Gulf Breeze must be efficient, Kenny surmised. It'd been a month since the three of them met with Karen and Lucy and no further crossword clues. He didn't know what to make of that long gap and was too skeptical to let himself think the mystery puzzler had given up. More likely that the *I'm Your Neighbor* gatherings held the past two weeks had a temporary chilling effect.

The gatherings were the brainchild of Joyce, who was in her element. The former PR pro was the behind-the-scenes coordinator for the well-attended gatherings that offered short programs and refreshments. "Feed them and they will come" she promised, and they did. Lucy was the primary hostess and emcee. She opened the sessions, introduced Karen who greeted the residents/neighbors, then turned it back over to Lucy.

What followed was an *Ask the Administrator* question-and-answer segment during which residents were encouraged to inquire (complain) about the meals, lobby for warmer or cooler thermostat settings in the common areas of Gulf Breeze, recommend to add or to eliminate field trips, etc. "Verbal bitch sessions" is how Joyce described this part of the program privately to Kenny and Frank. Karen, Lucy, and other staffers in attendance would respond to the questions and suggestions as appropriate.

A popular agenda item was the aptly named *Who am I?* segment. Lucy would describe an unnamed resident and at the end of her spiel the first person to correctly guess who it was would win a gift basket. Criteria for consideration varied but usually included how long they'd been Gulf Breeze residents, hobbies, male or female, height, and whatever else about the person Lucy could compile in advance.

To get the ball rolling, Lucy asked Kenny to be the subject of an early gathering. Nobody guessed correctly, and an awkward silence ensued until she mentioned that this resident loves crossword puzzles. A handful of people blurted out "Puzzle Man", which would have meant a tie and additional gift baskets that weren't in the budget. Lucy said the tiebreaker would be the resident's given name. It was Blackjack who bellowed "Kenny Puzzle Man Boone" and won the basket. He winked at Kenny when he came forward to claim his assortment of fruit, cheese, and crackers.

The business portion of the gatherings came after the attendees had snacks and settled into their seats. Brief presentations were made by staffers on personal hygiene, exercise, diet, and conflict resolution, and other topics. It always ended with the importance of asking for help and responding to neighbors in need. The goal, according to Joyce, was for the residents to leave the gatherings with awareness of their own and their neighbors' well-being. *Speak up, reach out* they were told.

"This is a subtle and hopefully effective way to reach the mystery puzzler," said Joyce. "We call it 'planting the seed'. Give the puzzler something to think about and maybe come forward. We shall see."

Whether the gatherings would eventually flush out the mystery puzzler was unknown to Kenny and his team as well as the staff. What was happening, much to the delight of Karen and Lucy, was a shift in the prevailing mood of the residents. There was less talk about the why three residents were so interested in the personal lives of other residents. Joyce said the conversational diversion was working as designed. Bottom line was the general population was gradually moving on to other things to talk about. She explained that the dynamics in a group living situation were fluid: what was a hot topic today might be replaced by another tomorrow.

"That's good and well, but you don't plan on holding the gatherings indefinitely, do you?" said Kenny in Karen's office with the others. "What do we do when the gatherings end?"

Karen said she didn't know, but Joyce was working on it. "Let's enjoy the respite from the rash of rumors we had just a couple of weeks ago. Our plan is working and it's getting back to normal around here, the way we like it."

Kenny looked at Frank, who shook his head. "Listen," said Kenny, "you can have *Who am I?* quizzes until everyone at Gulf Breeze has been the subject, or you run out of gift baskets. Until we figure out who the mystery puzzler is, the rest is just window dressing. Sorry, Joyce."

Lucy could barely contain herself waiting for a chance to speak. She made the point that it was more than window dressing, it was an example of social science in action.

"We're steering our residents away from a conspiracy theory toward better awareness of health and happiness," she said. "Have you seen how people are talking to each other more than ever? This is fantastic."

Frank gave kudos to Joyce and the Gulf Breeze staff for implementing *I'm Your Neighbor*. "It's a great program, we can all see the good it's doing. But let's not forget the reason we even have it is because of the mystery puzzler. And that's still going on as far as we know. What can we do about that?"

Of course, there was no easy answer, they agreed. Kenny reminded them that just because there hadn't been a puzzle message lately didn't mean they should consider the matter moot.

"We discussed early on that the *I'm Your Neighbor* gatherings could provide the mystery puzzler with resources to get help, or simply drive him or her underground. We don't know, do we? I don't necessarily take it as a good sign the messages have stopped. In fact, it worries me."

Karen chuckled. "I'm still getting to know you, Mr. Boone, but I've decided you're a cautious and skeptical man. That makes sense to me since you were career military. Plan your work and work your plan, right? Around here we savor our victories. Improved morale and increased socialization are two big ones."

Easy for you to say, Kenny thought to himself. There's one resident who, if you believe the clues, isn't savoring a victory.

"Sure," Kenny said. "We can all pat ourselves on the back. I'd trade that for the opportunity to extend a hand to the mystery puzzler and ask how I could help. Now that would be something to savor."

Chapter 64

Dr. Kim was perplexed. She'd heard from Karen that a personal matter with the unusual name of "mystery puzzler" had been a source of stress and angst for Kenny during the past year. The matter had recently come to the attention of and taken over by Gulf Breeze management.

It was an aha moment for the doctor because she had seen no indication that Kenny's stress level had been diminishing. If anything, the frequency of his dementia episodes–fogs– were occurring more often over time, which could be attributed to rising stress. The pieces now were falling into place for her. Miffed that no one had ever mentioned "mystery puzzler" when Kenny's health management plan was discussed, she assumed correctly that it was Kenny's secret until recently.

Kenny was nearing the end of a two-day stay at Galveston County Memorial Hospital where Dr. Kim had him admitted after he was observed in the game room with his face a mere six inches from the television... it was off. A small crowd had gathered around Kenny who was staring at the dark TV screen and carrying on a garbled conversation with... nobody. A housekeeper walking by saw what was going on and made a beeline for the nurses' station.

"Kenny, how are you feeling today?" Dr. Kim said. Sarah stood at the foot of the bed nervously watching.

He made an effort to sit up and got nowhere for his efforts. Dr. Kim told him to lay still while she activated the bed's adjustment controls. Once situated, he looked around and asked where he was.

Dr. Kim explained how he came to be at the hospital. Kenny listened with an incredulous expression on his face. He rested his chin on his chest and sighed.

"I don't remember anything," he said. "I was talking to a TV set? My God, what is happening to me?"

Sarah moved next to her father and took his hand. "Dad, you had another fog. Thankfully you were at Gulf Breeze where help was available. The EMTs brought you to the hospital and Dr. Kim came right over."

"Sarah is correct," said Dr. Kim. "You experienced a significant dementia episode triggered, we suspect, by a mini stroke. We're waiting for the result of an MRI you had last night. That will tell us exactly what's going on."

When Kenny repeated the words mini stroke, Dr. Kim described the incident for his and Sarah's benefit. She explained that in a mini stroke, the brain experiences a temporary lack of blood flow. On its own it doesn't cause permanent disabilities but could trigger a dementia episode.

"Dad, you were supposed to reduce stress. Instead you've added stress with the mystery puzzler ordeal," said Sarah. "Karen explained it to Dr. Kim and me. How could you have kept that from us for so long? You were just hurting yourself."

Kenny asked for a sip of water and then asked Sarah if he'd ever told her about a young airman in his unit at Royal Air Force Lakenheath in the United Kingdom. She said she couldn't recall him having done so. Dr. Kim decided to stay and listen. Perhaps the story would shed light on how his involvement with the mystery puzzler came to be.

"I was about 22 at the time, my first assignment overseas. There was a fellow there named Raymond Jorgensen, a handsome blond kid from Oshkosh, Wisconsin. We all thought he was a lady's man...he must be with his looks. Long story short, he was a closet homosexual. I figured it out and so did others. The teasing and name calling got ugly. This was the mid-1950s. Things were much different then. When Ray's repeated requests for a transfer were denied, he went AWOL, was returned to the base in handcuffs, and ultimately booted out of the Air Force with a dishonorable discharge."

Kenny took another sip of water and wiped his mouth with the back of his hand.

"I was called as a character witness at Ray's hearing. I can still see the look in his eyes as I testified. It went from hopeful to disappointed to despondent. I played it safe...barely acknowledged we knew each other when actually we were buddies. I was a coward, I chickened out. I could have helped save his career. He was counting on me and I did nothing."

Kenny closed out his story by saying that he was told at the time that Ray wasn't discharged for being gay; it was because he went AWOL. He never heard from or about Ray again.

"I promised myself that I'd never betray the trust of another person as long as I lived. The mystery puzzler, whoever it is, chose me for some reason. I was not going to betray that trust by running to authorities, at least until I knew more. This was my chance at redemption for crapping on Raymond Jorgensen. I stand by my actions; stress level be damned."

Dr. Kim stood and slung her briefcase over one shoulder. "I can't argue with your motive," she said. "My understanding from Karen is that the mystery puzzler case has been turned over to Gulf Breeze administration. Let them run with it. Now you can refocus on lowering stress. For real this time, okay?"

Kenny was tired and no longer interested in debating his actions with Dr. Kim or Sarah. He nodded in resignation and silently willed them to leave his hospital room.

No way am I going to recuse myself from the puzzle investigation. There will be an ending point sooner or later. Until that time, I'm still on duty... for the mystery puzzler, Raymond Jorgensen, and myself. Redemption.

Chapter 65

Table 14 was surprised to see Kenny at breakfast so soon after returning from the hospital. Blackjack suggested that Puzzle Man got used to being waited on at Galveston County and now demanded 24-hour room service at Gulf Breeze.

"I bet the hospital food is better than this," he said, shoving his bowl of bran flakes aside. "Just once I wish they'd cook me up a breakfast burrito and grits. A little hot sauce on both and I'm ready to go."

Frank was ready with a speedy comeback: "A little hot sauce and you're ready to go, all right. Straight to the bathroom. We all know you can't handle spicy food."

"Ha ha," Blackjack chortled. "I bet you were a regular Don Rickles with your jarhead buddies."

Kenny explained that the level of service he now received did include three meals a day delivered to his room. It came with a price, however. The meals, physical therapy, frequent check-ins by the nursing staff, and even the occasional escort to the vacant lot where he and Frank flew his drone airplane cost extra.

"So, do you get a rent credit this morning because you came down to the dining room?" Blackjack wanted to know.

"No, it doesn't work that way," Kenny replied. "Once you sign up for special services, you pay for them whether you use them or not. You have laundry done for you and Maisey? That's a flat weekly charge. Makes no difference if you decide to live in dirty clothes."

Blackjack grunted and pushed back from the table. He held a glass of juice for his wife to take a final sip and gently wiped her mouth. When they departed Frank turned to Kenny and commented that despite his often outlandish behavior, Blackjack was a gentle and caring man. Frank said he'd noticed that as well.

Kenny cleared his throat and wished for the millionth time that Rebecca was still alive. He knew that Frank felt the same way about his late wife.

"Here you go, my friend." Frank placed a pile of daily newspapers on Kenny's coffee table. "You probably aren't aware that Lucy added extra copies of *Galveston Daily News* to Gulf Breeze's subscription. It makes up for the one I take every morning for you."

"Nice of her to do that and nice of you to bring them to me," said Kenny. "Your timing is impeccable 'cause I'm caught up."

"Before you dig into the puzzles, I want to ask you how you're doing. No medical jargon, no glass is half-full response to pass the depression test, only you being straight with me. Airman to Marine. Two old dudes who don't tolerate BS. Brother to brother."

Kenny gave his friend a crooked smile. It had become noticeably more distorted since the episode that put him in the hospital a few weeks ago. He considered what Frank said and figured that after all he'd been through it was time to share his feelings with someone else. Not Sarah: he wanted to protect her as long as possible. Frank was the right person. What was the term used by the VA shrinks during counseling session? Oh yeah, *catharsis*.

"I'll tell you what I'm thinking if you tell me about Joyce. Is there a romance in the works?"

Frank confirmed that a romance wasn't in the works. He said he was fine with the way the relationship turned out. Seems that Joyce's initial attraction to him was tied to the mystery puzzler investigation. She was itching to get in on it and relive her glory days in corporate PR. Frank said he was her access point to the investigation. Beyond that they got along well and were friends, but nothing more.

"When Karen and Lucy relieved us of duty, Joyce became an unpaid PR advisor for Gulf Breeze," said Frank. "We still talk and share a coffee from time to time, but she's moved on. Unless you've taken a shine to a special someone here, it's just you and me again, Kenny."

Kenny had no problem with that. The last thing he needed was an old folks' home romance. Besides, he was honest enough with himself to admit that since his big stroke he wasn't much of a catch. He never told anyone about being self-conscious due to his muscle and speech impairments. It bothered him a lot.

"Do I need to remind you that what I say next stays between us?" Kenny realized that as soon as the words were out of his mouth, he'd made a mistake. "Sorry, I take it back. Dumb question."

He asked Frank another question: "Did you ever notice how whenever you have a checkup with your doctor, you're asked if you are depressed or have suicidal thoughts? At our age we get that all the time. Here's where I am on that one."

Kenny took a deep breath and let it out. He rambled a bit but managed to say what he was feeling. Frank was patient and refrained from interrupting.

"I tell the doctor that I don't believe I'm clinically depressed; however, I do get depressed frequently. For example, when I have a bad day due to pain and difficulty getting around. Or when I think about Rebecca. Or when I realize I'll probably die here and not at my real home. And being lonely. And more recently, I get depressed when I think about the mystery puzzler. I worry that I'll have a fog or another stroke and never be able to help the puzzler. Do I sound suicidal?"

Frank didn't think Kenny seemed suicidal. He sounded like most of the other residents of Gulf Breeze, in the homestretch of life with a lot of time to think about things. The longer you live, Frank said, the more you have to think about: accomplishments, missed opportunities, relationships, career, family life... regrets.

"I'm sure that's why all of the experts say it's important for us geezers to stay active and involved. I agree, but some days you just don't have the energy."

Kenny couldn't keep his eyes open. Frank stared at his friend and started to speak again but stopped when Kenny's head fell back on the recliner. Snoring was immediate. He picked up the stack of newspapers and took them to the hall closet where Kenny stored his notes on the mystery puzzler. He saw a file folder labeled "Clues" and opened it.

The first document in the file was a hand-printed copy of the clues that Kenny had turned over to Karen and Lucy. Beneath it were the newspapers with the original eleven clues. Frank realized he'd never seen the originals, only the separate list Kenny maintained.

He leafed through the old newspapers and read each clue, comparing them with the master list. They were all there. Something was off, though. Frank went back and forth between the master list and its newspaper counterparts. He removed his pocketed smart phone and snapped photos for future scrutiny. Kenny had coughed and Frank didn't want to be discovered snooping in his closet.

Frank placed a blanket over Kenny and turned out the overhead light before he left the room. His head was spinning as he walked back to his own room. All of a sudden, he had a new project to work on. He didn't have a good feeling about what it might lead to, and in fact was concerned that it'd be a source of significant depression for Kenny.

Damn, Frank thought as he hurried down the hallway with key in hand. *Is it asking too much to get good news for a change?*

Frank was gone when I awoke from my nap. I vaguely remember what I told him about myself. I hope I didn't come across like a cry baby. It sure felt good to unload pent up emotions. If Frank has similar feelings, he does a masterful job at hiding them. One day soon I'm going to pay back his kindness by asking him to tell me how he's doing... really doing.

I turned 85 recently. A milestone they tell me. Sarah brought a cake over for table 14. It was delicious. Even Maisey had a small piece fed to her by Blackjack. The man never fails to impress me with such tenderness toward his wife. A shame there isn't enough goodwill to carry over to temper his persona as a wise guy. Probably a defense mechanism to mask his own insecurities. We all have issues so I'm not going to judge him.

Dr. Kim believes the main contributor to my stress now is gone. She is wrong about that. I still spend a lot of time poring over my notes and scrutinizing the puzzle clues. I don't know what I expect to happen. I doubt that one day the identity of the puzzler will suddenly become crystal clear. My notes won't change and constantly reviewing them won't alter the content.

I need more time, but time is running out. If the puzzler managed to figure out that I added

Frank and Joyce to the team, then he or she (I'm tired of saying that) should know my fogs and strokes are taking me out of the race. Maybe the puzzler should pick a new recipient of the clues. Frank would be a logical choice.

I'll eat in my room tonight. The Rockets are playing the Lakers, which is always a hard fought basketball game. Think I'll multi-task by watching the game and working on the puzzles Frank brought me. I'm Puzzle Man and need to live up to my nickname.

Chapter 66

Kenny was tempted to dub them the "Dirty Dozen," but at the last moment showed restraint. He didn't want to diminish the importance of what was now the twelfth message left by the mystery puzzler: *so weary.*

"I'm surprised you called a meeting since you're no longer involved with this puzzler situation," said Karen. "Please tell me you and Frank haven't come out of retirement and are back in the fray."

Karen, Lucy, Joyce, and Frank stared at him. Frank, of course, already knew the purpose of the meeting and was ready to read the reactions of the others when Kenny said his piece.

"After a fairly long spell with no new clues, number twelve was left for me in the newspaper yesterday. It was *so weary.* I'm no expert, but it sounds like the puzzler is growing tired of the whole thing. Either that means it's ending, or a climax is coming."

Lucy said she was surprised about the latest clue considering the runaway success of the *I'm Your Neighbor* gatherings. Frank didn't recall seeing that clue on any of the recent batch of puzzles he delivered to Kenny's room and assumed he missed it.

"Obviously the gatherings and clues aren't mutually exclusive," said Karen. "They're separate but related. However, even with the new clue I'm not going to authorize that we resume the interviews with residents."

Kenny said he had no intention of talking about the puzzle clues to any resident, even the final four, unless they came to him first. As far as he and Frank were concerned, they were still in wait-and-see mode.

"I'm glad to hear that," said Karen. "Joyce suggested we continue *I'm Your Neighbor'* for another two months and then evaluate its effectiveness. Perhaps we'll offer them monthly rather than weekly. We'll do a survey and see what's what."

The meeting ended and Kenny and Frank walked out together. Kenny wondered if Frank had something he wanted to say.

"Yes, as a matter of fact I have two things rattling around in my head. First, I hope you don't obsess about the twelfth clue. Stress! You said at the meeting you'd wait and see where the clue led. Stick to that, okay?"

Kenny gestured toward the always busy bistro. "I'll try my best, that's all I can do." They stood in line for coffee then took their drinks to the patio. Their usual table was occupied so they found an open bench. Kenny prompted Frank to get to the second thing on his mind.

"Right, you said something about a mystery involving Barbara and Herb. Is it related to the mystery puzzler? They were both on the short-list as I recollect."

Kenny said they both were on the list, but Herb's name was removed not when he died, rather when the latest clue was revealed. With a wry grin, Kenny muttered that dead men leave no clues, and then acknowledged that Barbara was still a contender.

"It could be Barbara, but I'm not convinced she's the one," said Kenny. "Here's another piece of information for you to keep confidential: she confessed to me that when Herb was suffering his heart attack, she didn't try to help him. She simply watched him writhe on the floor until he stopped moving. That's when she called 9-1-1."

Frank was perplexed. "So, she panicked and froze. We've both seen men do that in combat. I wouldn't call that a confession."

"You weren't there, Frank. Barbara told me she made a conscious decision to do nothing. She finally was in control and loved it. Trust me, she's glad Herb died."

Frank jumped right to the obvious conclusion, that she was the mystery puzzler.

"Think about it, she'd been harboring dark thoughts about her husband and finally acted on them. She knew what she was capable of doing and reached out to you for help. Don't you see it?"

Kenny had seen it at the time she told him about Herb's fatal heart attack. Upon reflection, though, he came to believe that she was riddled with guilt. She simply froze and by the time she gathered her wits it was too late. Nothing pre-meditated about it.

"Maybe you're right. After all, you were the one she opened up to," said Frank. "The clincher is there was another clue left after Herb died. It's got to be from someone else. This is maddening."

Kenny nodded. "Tell me about it. This is a good example of why I can't let go of the mystery puzzler affair. It's become a calling for me, much to the disapproval of Sarah, Dr. Kim, Karen, Lucy, and even you. Only you know what I'm keeping bottled up."

Frank offered to talk with Joyce and ask her to get closer to Barbara. He said that Barbara might be more apt to speak freely to another woman, a widow herself. Joyce could use her communication skills to dig deeper than Kenny or he could ever do.

"I'm willing to let Joyce have a go at it as long as she isn't told about the circumstances of Herb's final moments," said Kenny. "I don't want her to be in a position of proving or disproving what we've told her about Herb and Barbara. It'll mean more if it comes out naturally. You know, girl talk. Besides, I promised Barbara I'd be discreet."

"I see your point," said Frank. "I'll handle this with kid gloves. Joyce won't be told why we want her to become Barbara's new buddy. Should we tell Karen and Lucy?"

Kenny's vote was to keep all of this between the two of them. It was hearsay from an emotional widow, so why spread a rumor that could be devastating to Barbara? Frank saw the logic in Kenny's opinion and got up to go find Joyce.

"Hold up a moment, will you Frank? As a new airman based far from home, I was approached by a seasoned NCO who read the loneliness in my demeanor and gave me sound advice. He said in life you really only need a few good friends to be happy. You can have dozens of acquaintances, but friends were the real key.

"I always remembered his advice. Now, decades later, I realize I really only need one good friend. That's you, Frank."

Frank was touched. "I feel the same way about you, Kenny. You may want to make more friends here because I won't be around forever."

Frank grimaced when Kenny softly said, "Just be around longer than me."

Frank hadn't seen Kenny in almost four days. He was worried and had a right to be. This was the longest stretch of time his friend hadn't come to the dining room for a meal or showed up in the game room to work a crossword puzzle. Frank stopped by room 103 often and noted that one of several nurses on rotating shifts was always inside. Once he saw Sarah and tapped on the door to get her attention.

"Hi, Frank, the nurses told me you've been coming around. Come on in. Dad's asleep in his room. He's getting water and nourishment intravenously. If he's not in a coma, he's close to it."

"What happened? He seemed fine on Monday."

Sarah explained that a nurse checked in on him Tuesday morning and he was sound asleep. So, she came back at noon and he'd barely moved. That's when she put a call into Dr. Kim who ordered him to be connected to the IVs and have 24-hour nursing support.

Frank stared at the closed bedroom door and sighed. Sarah was sniffling and wiping her eyes. He put an arm around her shoulders and tried to find the right words to say to her. Every time he began to speak the lump in his throat got in the way.

Sarah told Frank she'd planned to stop at table 14 and update Blackjack and Maisey at dinner but didn't really feel up to it. Frank said he'd do it that evening and for her not to give it another thought. He got permission to check on Kenny before he left and stuck his head inside the door.

"Hang in there, Kenny, we're all pulling for you to get better. I want you to give me another flying lesson before the humidity gets too unbearable. And don't worry about the daily crossword puzzles... I'm saving them for you. Please wake up."

On the fifth day, Kenny awoke alone in his darkened room. He tried to rise, but found he was confined by wires and tubes and what he recognized as a dreaded catheter. Despite a dry mouth and throat, he managed to croak "What the hell?" loud enough for the nurse to hear him through the wall.

By mid-afternoon Kenny had eaten, showered, and dressed. The IVs were gone per Dr. Kim's orders. The around-the-clock presence of nurses was changed to periodic check-ins. Kenny walked a couple of laps around the first floor and ended up in the game room. People looked at him like he was a rock star or more likely had just returned from the dead. Peculiar to him because he had absolutely no memory of the past five days.

Frank sat down next to him, out of breath and red in the face. He said he'd just come from Kenny's room and was surprised to see it empty. He quick-walked to the lobby area nearly mowing down a man on crutches who decided to change directions without signaling.

"Here you are," said Frank. "I see you decided to stop doing your Rip Van Winkle impersonation."

"Hello, Frank. "Did you have a few Bloody Marys for breakfast 'cause I don't know what you're talking about. I'm waiting for today's newspaper so I can do the crossword, just like I do every morning."

Frank pointed out that it was three-thirty in the afternoon and the newspaper was up in his room along with the past four days' copies. He'd deliver them to Kenny shortly. Frank didn't know what to make of Kenny's comment, if he was being coy or actually couldn't remember the recent past.

"C'mon, are you telling me you don't realize you've been in bed for four days, hooked up to IVs? I was worried that you may never wake up it went on so long."

Kenny hadn't been teasing Frank. He couldn't recall anything of what had been his most lengthy fog yet. According to Dr. Kim, this dementia episode made the others pale by comparison. She said she was gravely concerned that was the precursor to additional, major episodes that would further affect his memory.

"Okay, Kenny, today's a new day," said Frank. "Let's look forward and not backward. You want to talk about Barbara and the mystery puzzler?"

Kenny looked at him with a blank stare. Frank wondered if Kenny had forgotten about both. He thought to himself that if so it'd be a good thing to improve Kenny's stress level and overall health. But then the blank expression was replaced by one of alertness.

"Yes, of course. Any new clues lately?"

"No, not since the *so weary* clue. It's been pretty quiet. We can expect a briefing from Joyce about Barbara any time. In fact, I just saw her in the lobby area. I'll see if she's still around. Be right back."

Frank found Joyce waiting for the Gulf Breeze shuttle to take a group of residents on a shopping outing. She glanced at her watch and told Frank she had about ten minutes to spare.

"Good to see you up and about again, Kenny," said Joyce. "I'll make this quick 'cause the van leaves in a few minutes."

Joyce summarized her conversations with Barbara by saying that there was no indication she was the mystery puzzler and that they might as well remove her from the suspects list.

"My thoughts exactly," said Kenny. "Anything else about her you found to be curious or... interesting?"

"It would be helpful if you told me what you were after so I could be on the lookout for 'tells' that would allow me to dig deeper in our conversations. But I'm sure you have your reasons. Anyway, she certainly seems in good spirits so soon after Herb's passing.

"As to your last question about Barbara, I detect something is up with her. What I mean is she is very guarded in her remarks, like she is covering up for something. Kind of spooky if you ask me. Want me to make another go at her? Try to see why she's so careful and tentative?"

Kenny and Frank looked at each other before Kenny replied. "No, drop it. I had a hunch about Barbara, and it didn't go anywhere. Thanks for talking to her. From this point on please just keep it friendly, casual, and supportive. She's still working through the grieving process."

Joyce went to catch the shuttle and Frank complimented Kenny on how he handled Joyce's task of talking to Barbara.

"You did the right thing," said Frank. "No point in getting more involved in Barbara's guilt about her husband. She needs to heal and move on. By the way, your memory seems fine to me. How can you not know you slept for four days straight?"

Kenny said the fog must have been significant if they had to put him on a catheter. He temporarily cut out coffee because it was painful to urinate.

"Tell me about it," laughed Frank. "I had a catheter when kidney stones were removed. I still shudder thinking about that."

"You're what, 83 years old?" said Kenny. "Wait till you get to be 85 like me, then you'll know what being an old fart is all about."

Chapter 68

Frank thanked everyone for attending the meeting on short notice. Dr. Kim, Sarah, Karen, and Lucy waited patiently to learn why they were seated around a large table at a nearby Denny's instead of in the Gulf Breeze conference room.

"What I have to say is personal and disturbing to me," he said. "Meeting at Gulf Breeze would be noticed, and Kenny might have found out we met without him. I wanted to avoid that from happening."

Karen said he had their full attention and urged him to get to the point.

"The point, yes, the point. "I know the identity of the mystery puzzler."

They fired questions at Frank until he held up his hand. He confirmed it was not one of the final four suspects, which surprised them all.

"It's Kenny, he's the mystery puzzler," said Frank. This time there was total silence. Frank took advantage of the lull to push on with his rationale.

"It was a fluke, actually, how I figured it out. It occurred to me that no one ever saw the original newspaper crossword puzzles with the clues. All we got from Kenny was his hand-written list. Well, I was looking through his mystery puzzler notes a while back and found the newspapers. I compared the handwriting to his master list and guess what, they matched."

Sarah was the first to react. She was shocked at the news of her father. She asked the others if they thought it was some kind of joke he was playing. If so, she was terribly sorry.

"No, just the opposite," said Dr. Kim. "Your father believes with all his heart that the puzzle messages are from another resident. He's spent the past year consumed with uncovering the identity of this person when those messages are his own subconscious cries for help. There is no attempt to deceive–it's dementia. He is convinced that a resident chose him for assistance and it's his duty to come to the rescue."

Karen was relieved that the puzzler was no longer a mystery. She asked Lucy to get Joyce to help her prepare an announcement that would dispel any lingering rumors about "secret meetings with residents." Karen then turned to Dr. Kim and said she assumed the doctor would tactfully explain to Kenny that *he* was the mystery puzzler, which would put an end to the ordeal.

"No, absolutely not!" said Frank. "That would crush Kenny's spirit. Humiliate and drive him into depression. I'm no doctor, I'm his friend. I know Kenny. Please don't do this to him."

Dr. Kim said that Frank made a good point. There was no medical reason to confront Kenny with the potentially harmful news. She asked what Frank had in mind.

"He's losing his memory, right? And the fogs are becoming more frequent? He doesn't recall anything about his four-day sleep. I say we do nothing, tell nobody else. Let him hang onto the investigation; it gives him a reason to stay mentally active and engaged. No harm in that, right?"

Karen said she was okay with that approach if Dr. Kim, Sarah, and Lucy agreed. They each nodded. She urged Frank to convince Kenny not to approach residents in pursuit of exposing the puzzler. That would keep things stirred up. Frank said he'd manage that with Kenny by getting him to focus on the newspaper puzzle clues.

Frank and Sarah walked to the parking lot together. She thanked him profusely for looking out for her father.

He turned to her and said, "We're bros or bruhs, whatever the young people call brothers these days. We have each other's back."

Chapter 69

Sarah and Justin waited while Kenny finished the chili dog they'd brought to his room from Sonic drive-in. She saw the stack of mystery puzzler papers he'd been working on, filled with margin scribbles, and Post-it Notes. Puzzle Man's headquarters. Next to those papers was a three-ring binder with a piece of masking tape on the cover labeled *Diary. No way*, she thought. *Not Kenny Boone.*

Kenny could feel their eyes on him, so he acknowledged the elephant in the room.

"I'm not crazy, I'm old," he said. "Dr. Kim says my fogs are getting stronger and I have trouble remembering them among other things. Maybe that's good. Who wants to remember everything?"

Sarah asked if Kenny was at peace with living at Gulf Breeze after wanting to come home since the day he arrived. Kenny grunted and shrugged in noncommittal body language. Sarah was content not to get a resounding "no."

She said her birthday was coming up and wanted Kenny to attend her party if he was up to it. Perhaps at a local Mexican restaurant.

"Justin will be there along with a few of my close friends," she said. "I'd love to have Frank and even Lucy come, too."

"I wouldn't miss it for the world," said Kenny. "But I have two stipulations. First, I want to give you a special gift and I need you to tell me what you'd like. Second, I want to hold the party at my home so some more of my friends could stop by. Deal?"

"You mean my home? That's fine with me."

Kenny stood, indicated that Sarah and Justin should do the same, and wrapped his arms around them.

"I mean *my* home, here at Gulf Breeze. It took me a long while, but this is where I belong. At peace? Yes. Happy? Working on it. Now what about that special gift?"

Sarah wiped her eyes and told him that he'd just given it to her.